Wicked Wolf

Also from Carrie Ann Ryan:

Wicked Wolf

A Redwood Pack Novella

By Carrie Ann Ryan

1001 Dark Nights

EVIL EYE
CONCEPTS

Wicked Wolf
A Redwood Pack Novella
By Carrie Ann Ryan

1001 Dark Nights

Published by Evil Eye Concepts, Incorporated

Acknowledgments From The Author

To Liz. Thank you for saying hello at Coastal Magic and starting everything I never knew I wanted. You took a chance on an author who smiled and loved wolves. You are my rock star and I count myself lucky to know you, love you, and read with you. Thank you for loving the Redwood Pack as much (if not more) than I do.

Also, dear readers, thank you for being with me for the first step, every step since, and the steps to come.

Sign up for the 1001 Dark Nights Newsletter
and be entered to win a Tiffany Key necklace.

There's a contest every month!

Go to www.1001DarkNights.com to subscribe.

As a bonus, all subscribers will receive a free
1001 Dark Nights story
The First Night
by Lexi Blake & M.J. Rose

One Thousand and One Dark Nights

Once upon a time, in the future...

I was a student fascinated with stories and learning.
I studied philosophy, poetry, history, the occult, and
the art and science of love and magic. I had a vast
library at my father's home and collected thousands
of volumes of fantastic tales.

I learned all about ancient races and bygone
times. About myths and legends and dreams of all
people through the millennium. And the more I read
the stronger my imagination grew until I discovered
that I was able to travel into the stories... to actually
become part of them.

I wish I could say that I listened to my teacher
and respected my gift, as I ought to have. If I had, I
would not be telling you this tale now.
But I was foolhardy and confused, showing off
with bravery.

One afternoon, curious about the myth of the
Arabian Nights, I traveled back to ancient Persia to
see for myself if it was true that every day Shahryar
(Persian: شهریار, "king") married a new virgin, and then
sent yesterday's wife to be beheaded. It was written
and I had read, that by the time he met Scheherazade,
the vizier's daughter, he'd killed one thousand
women.

Something went wrong with my efforts. I arrived in the midst of the story and somehow exchanged places with Scheherazade – a phenomena that had never occurred before and that still to this day, I cannot explain.

Now I am trapped in that ancient past. I have taken on Scheherazade's life and the only way I can protect myself and stay alive is to do what she did to protect herself and stay alive.

Every night the King calls for me and listens as I spin tales. And when the evening ends and dawn breaks, I stop at a point that leaves him breathless and yearning for more. And so the King spares my life for one more day, so that he might hear the rest of my dark tale.

As soon as I finish a story... I begin a new one... like the one that you, dear reader, have before you now.

Chapter One

There were times to drool over a sexy wolf.

Sitting in the middle of a war room disguised as a board meeting was not one of those times.

Gina Jamenson did her best not to stare at the dark-haired, dark-eyed man across the room. The hint of ink peeking out from under his shirt made her want to pant. She *loved* ink and this wolf clearly had a lot of it. Her own wolf within nudged at her, a soft brush beneath her skin, but she ignored her. When her wolf whimpered, Gina promised herself that she'd go on a long run in the forest later. She didn't understand why her wolf was acting like this, but she'd deal with it when she was in a better place. She just couldn't let her wolf have control right then—even for a man such as the gorgeous specimen a mere ten feet from her.

Today was more important than the wants and feelings of a half wolf, half witch hybrid.

Today was the start of a new beginning.

At least that's what her dad had told her.

Considering her father was also the Alpha of the Redwood Pack, he would be in the know. She'd been adopted into the family when she'd been a young girl. A rogue wolf during the war had killed her parents, setting off a long line of events that had changed her life.

As it was, Gina wasn't quite sure how she'd ended up in the meeting between the two Packs, the Redwoods and the Talons. Sure, the Packs had met before over the past fifteen years of their treaty, but this meeting seemed different.

This one seemed more important somehow.

And they'd invited—more like *demanded*—Gina to attend.

At twenty-six, she knew she was the youngest wolf in the room by far. Most of the wolves were around her father's age, somewhere in the hundreds. The dark-eyed wolf might have been slightly younger than that, but only slightly if the power radiating off of him was any indication.

Wolves lived a long, long time. She'd heard stories of her people living into their thousands, but she'd never met any of the wolves who had. The oldest wolf she'd met was a friend of the family, Emeline, who was over five hundred. That number boggled her mind even though she'd grown up knowing the things that went bump in the night were real.

Actually, she *was* one of the things that went bump in the night.

"Are we ready to begin?" Gideon, the Talon Alpha, asked, his voice low. It held that dangerous edge that spoke of power and authority.

Her wolf didn't react the way most wolves would, head and eyes down, shoulders dropped. Maybe if she'd been a weaker wolf, she'd have bowed to his power, but as it was, her wolf was firmly entrenched within the Redwoods. Plus, it wasn't as if Gideon was *trying* to make her bow just then. No, those words had simply been spoken in his own voice.

Commanding without even trying.

Then again, he *was* an Alpha.

Kade, her father, looked around the room at each of his wolves and nodded. "Yes. It is time."

Their formality intrigued her. Yes, they were two Alphas who held a treaty and worked together in times of war, but she had thought they were also friends.

Maybe today was even more important than she'd realized.

Gideon released a sigh that spoke of years of angst and worries. She didn't know the history of the Talons as well as she probably should have, so she didn't know exactly why there was always an air of sadness and pain around the Alpha.

Maybe after this meeting, she'd be able to find out more.

Of course, in doing so, she'd have to *not* look at a certain wolf in the corner. His gaze was so intense she was sure he was studying her. She felt it down in her bones, like a fiery caress that promised something more.

Or maybe she was just going crazy and needed to find a wolf to scratch the itch.

She might not be looking for a mate, but she wouldn't say no to something else. Wolves were tactile creatures after all.

"Gina?"

She blinked at the sound of Kade's voice and turned to him.

She was the only one standing other than the two wolves in charge of security—her uncle Adam, the Enforcer, and the dark-eyed wolf.

Well, *that* was embarrassing.

She kept her head down and forced herself not to blush. From the heat on her neck, she was pretty sure she'd failed in the latter.

"Sorry," she mumbled then sat down next to another uncle, Jasper, the Beta of the Pack.

Although the Alphas had called this meeting, she wasn't sure what it would entail. Each Alpha had come with their Beta, a wolf in charge of security…and her father had decided to bring her.

Her being there didn't make much sense in the grand scheme of things since it put the power on the Redwoods' side, but she wasn't about to question authority in front of another Pack. That at least had been ingrained in her training.

"Let's get started then," Kade said after he gave her a nod. "Gideon? Do you want to begin?"

Gina held back a frown. They *were* acting more formal than usual, so that hadn't been her imagination. The Talons and the Redwoods had formed a treaty during the latter days of the war between the Redwoods and the Centrals. It wasn't as though these were two newly acquainted Alphas meeting for the first time. Though maybe when it came to Pack matters, Alphas couldn't truly be friends.

What a lonely way to live.

"It's been fifteen years since the end of the Central War, yet there hasn't been a single mating between the two Packs," Gideon said, shocking her.

Gina blinked. Really? That couldn't be right. She was sure there had to have been *some* cross-Pack mating.

Right?

"That means that regardless of the treaties we signed, we don't believe the moon goddess has seen fit to fully accept us as a unit," Kade put in.

"What do you mean?" she asked, then shut her mouth. She was the youngest wolf here and wasn't formally titled or ranked. She should *not* be speaking right now.

She felt the gaze of the dark-eyed wolf on her, but she didn't turn to look. Instead, she kept her head down in a show of respect to the Alphas.

"You can ask questions, Gina. It's okay," Kade said, the tone of his voice not changing, but, as his daughter, she heard the softer edge. "And what I mean is, mating comes from the moon goddess. Yes, we can find our own versions of mates by not bonding fully, but a true bond, a true potential mate, is chosen by the moon goddess. That's how it's always been in the past."

Gideon nodded. "There haven't been many matings within the Talons in general."

Gina sucked in a breath, and the Beta of the Talons, Mitchell, turned her way. "Yes," Mitchell said softly. "It's that bad. It could be that in this period of change within our own pack hierarchy, our members just haven't found mates yet, but that doesn't seem likely. There's something else going on."

Gina knew Gideon—as well as the rest of his brothers and cousins—had come into power at some point throughout the end of the Central War during a period of the Talon's own unrest, but she didn't know the full history. She wasn't even sure Kade or the rest of the Pack royalty did.

There were some things that were intensely private within a Pack that could not—and should not—be shared.

Jasper tapped his fingers along the table. As the Redwood Beta, it was his job to care for their needs and recognize hidden threats that the Enforcer and Alpha might not see. The fact that he was here told Gina that the Pack could be in trouble from something *within* the Pack, rather than an outside force that Adam, the Enforcer, would be able to see through his own bonds and power.

"Since Finn became the Heir to the Pack at such a young age, it has changed a few things on our side," Jasper said softly. Finn was her brother, Melanie and Kade's oldest biological child. "The younger generation will be gaining their powers and bonds to the goddess earlier than would otherwise be expected." Her uncle looked at her, and she kept silent. "That means the current Pack leaders will one day not have the bonds we have to our Pack now. But like most healthy Packs, that doesn't mean we're set aside. It only means we will be there to aid the new hierarchy while they learn their powers. That's how it's always been in our Pack, and in others, but it's been a very long time since it's happened to us."

"Gina will one day be the Enforcer," Adam said from behind her. "I don't know when, but it will be soon. The other kids aren't old enough yet to tell who will take on which role, but since Gina is in her twenties, the shifts are happening."

The room grew silent, with an odd sense of change settling over her skin like an electric blanket turned on too high.

She didn't speak. She'd known about her path, had dreamed the dreams from the moon goddess herself. But that didn't mean she wanted the Talons to know all of this. It seemed…private somehow.

"What does this have to do with mating?" she asked, wanting to focus on something else.

Gideon gave her a look, and she lowered her eyes. He might not be her Alpha, but he was still a dominant wolf. Yes, she hadn't lowered her eyes before, but she'd been rocked a bit since Adam had told the others of her future. She didn't want to antagonize anyone when Gideon clearly wanted to show his power. Previously, everything had been casual; now it clearly was not.

Kade growled beside her. "Gideon."

The Talon Alpha snorted, not smiling, but moved his gaze. "It's fun to see how she reacts."

"She's my daughter and the future Enforcer."

"*She* is right here, so how about you answer my question?"

Jasper chuckled by her side, and Gina wondered how quickly she could reach the nearest window and jump. It couldn't be that far. She wouldn't die from the fall or anything, and she'd be able to run home.

Quickly.

"Mating," Kade put in, the laughter in his eyes fading, "is only a small part of the problem. When we sent Caym back to hell with the other demons, it changed the power structure within the Packs as well as outside them. The Centrals who fought against us died because they'd lost their souls to the demon. The Centrals that had hidden from the old Alphas ended up being lone wolves. They're not truly a Pack yet because the goddess hasn't made anyone an Alpha."

"Then you have the Redwoods, with a hierarchy shift within the younger generation," Gideon said. "And the Talons' new power dynamic is only fifteen years old, and we haven't had a mating in long enough that it's starting to worry us."

"Not that you'd say that to the rest of the Pack," Mitchell mumbled.

"It's best they don't know," Gideon said, the sounds of an old argument telling Gina there was more going on here than what they revealed.

Interesting.

"There aren't any matings between our two Packs, and I know the trust isn't fully there," Kade put in then sighed. "I don't know how to fix that myself. I don't think I can."

"You're the Alpha," Jasper said calmly. "If you *tell* them to get along with the other wolves, they will, and for the most part, they have. But it isn't as authentic as if they find that trust on their own. We've let them go this long on their own, but now, I think we need to find another way to have our Packs more entwined."

The dark-eyed wolf came forward then. "You've seen something," he growled.

Dear goddess. His voice.

Her wolf perked, and she shoved her down. This wasn't the time.

"We've seen…something, Quinn," Kade answered.

Quinn. That was his name.

Sexy.

And again, *so* not the time.

Gideon nodded. "Something is coming. Maybe not within the next year, but soon enough that we need to work on the foundations of our bonds if we want to persevere."

Gina sat back in her chair. She didn't have the connection the others had. She had only the glimpse into her future that spoke of her powers as the Enforcer. One day she'd stand by her father's side and help protect the Pack from outside forces. One day she'd gain new bonds to each wolf so she could protect them.

She'd be the first half witch, non-blood family member in the history of the Redwoods to do so.

That fact had led to tension within the Pack, but that was her problem. One she'd deal with later. Now she needed to focus on what was being said in front of her.

"So what do you propose?" Adam asked.

"We should form a council," Gideon answered. "But not one of wolves who want too much power and won't decide on anything but how to rise in the ranks without lifting a claw."

"Agreed," Kade said. "One the two Alphas will join in regularly. The council *will* answer to us because that is how power is handled. But the council will be focused on the Packs themselves and how they can work together."

"We didn't do this before because it was important to let them find their own way," Gideon said. "But I don't think we have that kind of time now."

"What kind of time are you talking about?" Quinn asked.

"A year? A decade? I don't know." Gideon sighed. "We live so many years that time is relative. And we're all going on a hunch right now, but the fact that we don't have matings between us, that's something at least."

Gina frowned and tried to understand what they were talking about.

"You both want to form a council between the two Packs. What would it entail? What kind of power would the council have if they have to answer to the Alphas? How would you choose who's on it? What would be their goal? This is a lot of change for Packs as old as ours, so how will you make sure that those who are *not* chosen will not be upset enough to do something to jeopardize it?"

Again, she shut her mouth. Damn her and her questions. She looked up at Quinn, who gave her an assessing glance. He looked impressed, but the expression came and went, so she could have been imagining it.

Instead, she looked over at Gideon to find him studying her. "I see why you brought her, Kade. She asks the right questions."

Gina held back a frown. "But do you have the answers?"

Dear God, Gina. Shut. Up.

Kade snorted. "We hope so. The council would not have the power to change laws or the way the hierarchy works. That's not how we rule. We are not humans. We are not a democracy. The Alpha's word is law."

Gideon growled in agreement.

"The council will be there to find a way for our two Packs to trust one another more," Kade continued. "If there are issues between individuals that need to be resolved, the council can find out what those are. I don't believe everyone is telling us everything when it comes to how they feel about the other Pack. I understand that. It was odd for us to form this treaty with one Pack while we were fighting another. The lack of true trust makes sense, but that doesn't mean we can allow it to continue. It's been too long for them to cling to their resentment."

Gideon nodded. "We joined with you right after I became Alpha. It was the first major decision in my new position, and not everyone agreed with me. It was a major gamble. We need to show the others that we can work together when the time comes and when it is needed. We are still two Packs and have two Alphas. That doesn't mean, though, that we need to fight over every little thing."

"We need to be able to stand united while retaining our own identities," Kade added. "Pack members who know the wolves in all generations, not just the older ones who have seen war, will be of an asset. If our submissives don't trust their dominants to protect them within the two Packs, then we are lost. *That* is what the council is for. We need to be able to shift with the future, and I don't think staying safe within our dens under the magic of wards will work forever."

Gina swallowed hard. The wards had broken once before. She didn't want to see that again. Her parents had died *within* the wards because of a traitor. When the wards had broken…that had been even worse.

"We are living in an age of technology, and we can't hide like we used to," Gideon said. "That is another part of the council. We need to be able to communicate with *all* Packs around the United States, not just between the two of us. If our plans work, that will be the next step."

Gina's eyes widened. "That's huge."

Quinn growled in front of her, and her wolf did a full body shiver. "That's something that cannot be accomplished with a few words and paltry promises."

"I know," Gideon said softly. "But we need to start somewhere. If we show the others within our own Packs that we have a sense of trust, it will help us. It's just one step in the process. We need a voice within the Packs that does not come from alpha authority. If the council can find ways for the Packs to work together on things *outside* of war, it will help when war comes."

Their words scared her; she wasn't going to lie. They'd had many years of relative peace, but that peace had been broken once before. Who's to say it wouldn't be broken again?

"I fear that if we don't do this, we'll lose everything we worked so hard for," Kade said before meeting Gideon's gaze. "The fact that you aided us in the war helped some people trust, but after the Centrals' demise, I'm afraid it will take more than war for that to continue."

Gideon nodded. "We had our own struggles, our own failures with our Pack. Fighting might help with the baser needs of our wolves, but actions that involve confidence but not dependence on the other Pack are the only things that can help bring true trust—and one day, hopefully, the moon goddess's favor."

"Who do you propose be on the council?" Jasper asked.

Kade tapped his fingers on the table. "Parker would be a good choice. He can mediate others with a sense of calm that I've not seen in many wolves."

Gideon's eyes widened marginally before he nodded.

Gina held back her own reaction. Parker was her cousin but, like her, hadn't been born into the Jamensons. He was only two years younger than her but seemed far older.

The fact that both Alphas wanted him as part of their council was a huge step. Not everyone trusted Parker because of the blood in his veins. Gina had always thought that was a crock of shit, but then again, not everyone trusted her because of her powers.

She was a fire witch, her powers inherited from her birth mother,

Larissa. But unlike her mother, she didn't have full control of her powers. The only other witch she knew, Hannah, was an earth witch and the Healer.

There was no one to train her, and if she was honest with herself, she was scared as well.

Not that she'd tell anyone else that.

They named three more wolves, so that there were two from each Pack. Gina didn't know the other Redwood, Farah, well, and had never met the two Talons, but that meant only that they weren't high in the hierarchy or friends of hers.

"As for leaders, we need one from each Pack to work as a unit," Gideon put in.

Kade nodded. "Agreed. I propose Gina."

She blinked, more than a little shocked. Yes, they'd invited her to the meeting, but she was going to be the Enforcer. Wasn't there a reason for not making pack hierarchy a requirement in the group?

Gideon nodded. "Good with me."

Kade met her gaze, and she lowered her eyes. "The council will not always be comprised of the same people. It will fluctuate. I trust you to do right by our Pack. When the other kids grow up, and you all find your new powers, we can re-evaluate the council. For now, it will be a good experience. For all of you."

She nodded, stunned at his trust, despite the witch blood running in her veins. Between her and Parker, they were the poster children for weird family trees within the Pack. But she would not betray her family's trust and dishonor them by saying no.

She wasn't sure she *could* say no.

"Quinn, one of my lieutenants, will round out the council," Gideon said.

A lieutenant. That made sense. While the Redwoods had enforcers, lowercase *e*, to protect the Alpha, the Talons had lieutenants. They were strong wolves, loyal to the core, and would put their body in front of a claw or bullet to protect their Alpha.

Gina swallowed hard and looked at Quinn. He didn't react. Instead, he stood there, his gaze on her intense, and for some reason, she felt anger...or something akin to it rolling over him. She didn't know what she'd done to cause that kind of reaction, but she didn't like it. The two of them would now have to stand side by side in order to find a way for the Packs to work together more than they already were.

They had to prove that the Packs could have faith in one another.

Her lusting after him and him looking like he wanted to growl at her for something or another wouldn't help anyone.

"So that's six people, three from each Pack," Kade said finally. "We don't know what's coming, only that we need to stand united."

"We can't move on unless we know that we can help every person within our Packs, even those who feel they don't have a voice," Gideon said softly.

"Our jobs as Betas mean we look for those," Jasper said, his eyes on Mitchell, who nodded.

"But that doesn't mean we can help everyone," Mitchell added.

"If we have an outlet for people who *want* the Packs to work together, then we're one step closer," Gina said, her wolf growling in approval.

Quinn narrowed his eyes. "Talking won't do much, but action will, even if that action is showing that we're in agreement after all these years."

"The Packs fought together in the war that almost killed us," Kade put in. "Now we need to show that, in times of peace, that collaboration is still needed."

"Agreed," Gideon said.

With that, they finalized their plans to tell the other new members of the council, and Gina stood up, her wolf needing to run. There was too much energy in the room, too many dominant males. She was a dominant wolf in her own right, but in this room, she knew she was most likely the lowest rank. That didn't mean she was weak. That just showed how much freaking power was actually in the room to begin with.

"Gina? You and Quinn go for a walk along the neutral perimeter," Kade ordered. "Get to know one another since the two of you are the leaders of this experiment."

Gina stood, forcing her knees not to shake. If her father knew about the very dirty, sweaty images rolling through her brain right then, he probably wouldn't have ordered her to undertake such a task.

"Come with me," Quinn said then stalked out of the room.

She raised a brow at Jasper. "Bossy much?"

Her uncle snorted then shook his head. "He's not a submissive wolf, that's for sure." He grinned. "Well, even submissives have a strong drive."

She rolled her eyes. "You're thinking of your mate, and now I'm going to tell Willow you called her submissive."

Her uncle narrowed his eyes. "Do that, and I'll tell Finn you're the one who stole his favorite shirt."

She held up her hands in surrender. "I won't mention it then." She grinned, knowing Jasper was only teasing. "I'd best be off to find Quinn since he's probably brooding or something outside."

"Watch yourself with that one, Gina," Gideon said, and she froze, surprised the Alpha would say anything like that.

"Excuse me?" she asked.

Gideon sighed. "He's a strong wolf. A good wolf. But he's not the same wolf he once was. It's not my story to tell, but don't antagonize him."

Kade growled, and she did the same.

"Don't threaten my daughter."

"Alpha, he didn't threaten me," she said, her voice cool. "He only warned a council wolf about a wolf she will be working with in the future. That's how I'm taking it." If she didn't, there might just be bloodshed, and that was *not* a good idea in this small room with no real escape.

Kade tore his gaze from Gideon's and met hers before giving her a nod.

Their family relationship was a slippery slope. She was the oldest of her generation, and therefore, the first to blend into the roles that suited them as adults, rather than children. It wasn't easy finding a balance. Finn might be eighteen and older than his years, but he wasn't allowed to be a part of many of the Pack decisions. That would be changing soon. Finn was, after all, the Heir to the Redwood Pack. His time would come.

With one last glance at the others, she left the room and looked for Quinn. She didn't have to go far since he was right outside the main door. He probably had heard everything, but his face didn't show it. Maybe he didn't care that his Alpha felt the need to warn her about him, but she didn't want to think of that too much. She had enough to worry about.

"Ready?" she asked, trying to keep her wolf at bay. For some reason, her wolf did not want to stay calm. Instead, the damn thing wanted to rub up against the man in front of her.

This was going to make for an interesting council.

Quinn nodded then started off toward the border.

Apparently, he wasn't much of a talker.

Well, too bad because she was.

"So, what do we need to discuss?"

Quinn shrugged. "Anything we need to discuss can happen at the meetings. We can have the first one tomorrow at the place the Alphas choose. I'll send you the information when I receive it."

Gina stopped in her tracks. This domineering side of him wasn't sexy. Well, not when he treated her like his secretary or something. Domineering in other places…

No.

Focus.

She held up her hand. "Whoa. Wait. The whole point of this council is to show cooperation and the good that came from the treaty. If you're going to act all growly and rude, that's not going to help."

Quinn glared. "You are a young wolf, and this is your first real assignment I suspect. You'll learn that not all things need to be done with roses and smiles."

Of all the arrogant things… Okay, so this wolf had already pissed her off and they hadn't even had the freaking meeting yet.

"You can't be that much older than me," she spat. "Your wolf doesn't feel as old as the others, so watch it. I'm not a submissive wolf who needs protection or to be told what to do. I'm a dominant. I'm the one who does the protecting. So if you have this false sense of who I am, then you should back up."

Quinn didn't say anything.

"Fine then. We'll meet at the place the Alphas tell us. Us. Get it? I won't need you to tell me anything. Now since this isn't doing anything but making me want to claw your face off, I'm going back. Thanks for the meeting, *Quinn*."

She stomped away, pissed that she'd let herself be baited. The wolf clearly didn't trust her for some reason, and that was the inherent problem in the Packs to begin with. She'd have to nip that in the bud and fix it. She would not let her Pack get hurt because one dumbass male didn't understand his place in the world.

It was a shame that he was such an asshole though. Her wolf liked his wolf.

A lot.

Thankfully, she listened to her brain, not her libido or her wolf when it came to her decisions because there was one thing for sure—she would *not* be spending much time with Quinn.

No matter the whimpers her wolf made…or Quinn's sexy bedroom eyes.

She was stronger than that.

Mostly.

Chapter Two

That blasted female.

Quinn Weston stomped toward his den, his hands fisted at his sides. That little pup of a woman had gotten on his very last nerve, and he had no idea why.

Well, he had an idea why, but those big eyes and sexy curves didn't mean a thing.

Sure, keep telling yourself that, Quinn.

He couldn't believe his Alpha had put him together with that little wolf. She couldn't be out of her twenties yet. Considering most wolves lived well into their hundreds, she was still a baby. Yeah, she was an adult and, from the feel of her, could shift into a dominant wolf, but she wasn't ready for what a council between Packs would entail.

She wasn't ready for what he'd give her if she gave him the chance. Sure, she might be strong, dominant, and sexy as hell, but she'd break under the weight of his dominance.

He stopped in his tracks, cursed, and then rubbed the bridge of his nose.

What the *hell* was he thinking?

Maybe he hadn't been with a woman in so long that he'd finally lost his goddamn mind. He didn't want that young girl who probably hadn't even seen a naked man outside of wolf hunts before.

He didn't even *like* her.

She asked too many questions and thought herself better than she was because of her family. She probably hadn't even had to work for her position. No, she was the Alpha's daughter; therefore, she could do what she wanted.

So what if the goddess had given her dreams of her future gift and role as an Enforcer? All that meant was, yet again, her family connections had given her the power and prestige.

She wasn't like him. She hadn't had to work for every scintilla of power and placement within the hierarchy as he had for his role as lieutenant. No, it had been given to her.

In the back of his mind, he knew he was just making excuses. He was only lying to himself because he actually admired the way her mind worked, the way her wolf pushed forward when needed. Her family connections might have helped with the goddess, but even then, the power wouldn't have shifted unless the wolf could handle it. In fact, she wasn't even related by blood to the Jamensons. She'd been adopted into the royal family.

He remembered that had happened during the Central War when the Talons had been dealing with their own turmoil. People had talked, gossiped, and tried to understand how the new Alpha of the Pack had been in his right mind when he adopted not only one, but two children. Wolves were usually very family-oriented. Orphaned children would have been adopted into a family. There was no way they would have been left alone. The fact that they'd been taken into the Jamensons without question though, was different.

Blood conquered all, or at least that's how some of the wolves thought. The fact that Gina and her brother, Mark, had been taken into the family with its attendant power and responsibility, was huge news. Not everyone had taken it well, although he hadn't heard of the children being treated poorly.

That didn't mean it hadn't happened though. For all he knew, Gina had fought for what she had because of it.

Damn. Now look at him, he was making excuses for her and trying to soothe hurt feelings, even though she wasn't even there.

He clearly needed to go on a run and forget the pretty-eyed wolf.

The pretty-eyed, hybrid wolf.

Oh yes, he'd heard more stories about her than about her brother. Mark hadn't gained any powers from his mother's witch blood while Gina had apparently gained enough to become a true hybrid.

Half wolf, half witch.

Yet he didn't know anything about her powers in that respect. He'd heard only whispers about strength and instability. That scared him even more. There was no way he wanted to work with a wolf he didn't understand, and now his Alpha had put him in the position to do just that.

Not that he wanted to spend time with her to understand her at all.

No. What he was going to do was deal with her on the council until she became the Enforcer, and then she'd leave. He didn't want to know her more than that. He didn't want to have to find out all of her secrets. He'd leave that to the others. He didn't need to know more about her because, honestly, he was afraid once he did, he'd want to know more. He didn't want to want her. He was stronger than whatever his wolf *thought* he wanted.

Now he needed to ensure his Pack was safe and if he had to work alongside the woman, then he'd grit his teeth through it.

Just the thought of not doing everything to protect his Alpha and Pack burned under his skin, and he growled. Now look what that damned woman was doing to him.

He cursed again and started moving toward his home. He'd caught a ride to the meeting with Mitchell and Gideon but had chosen to run back. The exertion hadn't worked on the aggravation as well as he'd have liked, but at least he wasn't ready to tear someone's throat out.

Or pound a certain wolf up against a wall.

He cursed. He needed to get that image out of his head. She wasn't for him. Frankly, no one was for him. He'd had his shot and had lost it when Helena walked away.

He snorted.

Walking away was such an inadequate term for what she'd done.

She'd broken their mating bond.

Quinn hadn't thought such a thing was even possible.

When wolves mated, they not only found someone to spend the rest of their forever with, but also someone who became a vital part of their soul. Their wolves bonded through the mating bite, and their humans bonded through sex, as long as the male came deep within her. There were only a few potential wolves, humans, and witches in the world that a wolf could mate with and the union be blessed by the goddess. The fact that the Talons hadn't had that within their own pack in years was troubling enough. The fact that his former mate had destroyed their connection made him feel as though he'd lost part of his life.

His wolf had lost his other half, and the man had lost much more. He'd lost the mother of his child, the woman of his heart, and his trust of all things with a future.

He'd lost half his soul when Helena had forcibly shattered their mating bond. He wasn't right for anyone—let alone a little wolf from another Pack.

There was no way he'd put himself in that position again.

Quinn left his shirt off after his run, his body slick with sweat. Some of the unattached female wolves he passed gave him the eye then looked away, scared. They should be scared. He wasn't whole anymore.

He ignored the stares from other packmates and made his way home. Walker would be there watching Jesse, so he needed to relieve him.

"Dad!" Jesse, his five-year-old son, ran to him as he shouted his name.

All of Quinn's negative thoughts disappeared, and he opened his arms to catch the little boy who had jumped into his arms like there was no tomorrow, with no worries that Quinn could or would ever drop him.

Jesse wrapped his little arms around Quinn's neck and held on tight. Quinn hugged him back then held Jesse on his hip so he could make his way back inside to a waiting Walker. He was the Healer of the Talon Pack, younger brother to Gideon, and also happened to be one of the Brentwood triplets. Between Walker, Brandon, and Kameron, the three guys pretty much had a firm hold on power and responsibility.

"Hey, buddy," Quinn said to his son, who bounced in his arms. They chatted about Jesse's day, or rather Jesse chatted and Quinn listened, soaking it all in. It was nice to see Jesse with so much energy and enthusiasm. Those days were becoming harder and harder to come by. He squeezed his son, careful of his strength.

When Helena had done the unthinkable and left the way she had, she'd not only shattered Quinn's world, but she had done something to their son as well. The woman had not only walked away from Quinn, but their newborn as well. Jesse hadn't been healthy from that day on.

Walker and Quinn had no idea how to fix it. Jesse was just...weak. He had trouble shifting to his wolf—something that scared the shit out of Quinn. Wolves weren't supposed to get colds or the flu, but Jesse did and often. It was as if when Helena left Quinn broken open, she'd stolen part of Jesse, too. The bond between mother and child wasn't as strong as a mating bond since the mother-child bond faded over time when the child grew up, but it was still crucial to the child. If a parent died, then the bond would sever, but the child would live a full life—if not a sad one.

Yet Jesse was different.

This whole situation was different.

His little boy was only five years old, and yet Quinn didn't know how much longer Jesse could hold on. It was tiring to be an active little pup. It was even more tiring when his body was fighting itself.

He held back his sigh then walked into his home. Walker leaned against the kitchen island, his large arms crossed over his even larger chest. While Quinn was one big wolf, the Brentwoods were even bigger. The other man's dark hair was usually cropped close to his head, but it looked as if the Healer hadn't had a cut in a while. Walker's younger sister, Brynn, would probably be after him with shears soon.

"Thanks for watching Jesse," Quinn said as he put his son down. Jesse gripped his leg then leaned into him. Quinn smiled down at his son and ran a hand over his soft brown hair.

"No problem. The little guy and I finished our book, so we're on the lookout for the next one. I'll download a good one soon."

Since Jesse got tired so easily, he couldn't go out and roughhouse with the other pups in the den. It killed Quinn inside that he couldn't let his son go out and be a normal little pup, but if he did, Jesse would just grow weaker faster.

He had no idea what to do, and the fact that no one had been through this before made him feel so damn helpless. Helena had not only killed a part of him when she'd left, she'd irrevocably changed the way their son would grow up.

He would never be able to forgive her for deciding that she didn't want to be a mate and mom anymore.

That was, if he could ever find her.

She'd run away and cut ties with the Pack by using a dark witch. That fucking witch and her powers had ruined everything in his life, and he was only now able to pick up the pieces.

Just another reason he wanted nothing to do with Gina. He didn't trust witches. Not when they had the power to hurt his son and any bond he might have had. He didn't know what Gina could do, nor did he want to bother learning. The more he learned about her, the more she could learn about him, which would give her more power to hurt those he loved.

He was done being a doormat for those who wanted something better.

That little Redwood wolf would just have to deal with him in meetings and then go home. He wouldn't be finding out more about her, wouldn't be learning how she worked or what she did in her free time.

He'd do his duty because his Alpha had ordered it, and then he'd leave.

He couldn't afford to follow the path his wolf seemed to want. Oh yes, he felt the way his wolf brushed up against his skin, wanting contact, wanting the brunette Redwood wolf.

Well, that wasn't going to happen. His wolf would just have to deal with the hand they'd been dealt five years ago. It had worked so far, and he wasn't going to chance fate and his son's life again.

"Daddy? Uncle Walker says you are going to be on a council. What's a council?" Jesse asked and Quinn bent down so he was at eye level with his son.

He ran a hand over Jesse's hair and smiled. "It's a group of wolves that works together for a common goal. I'm on one now with the Redwoods and some of the Talons you know."

Jesse nodded, his little face serious. "Do you think I can be on a council when I get older?"

Something inside Quinn clutched at the thought of his little boy older but he pushed it away. "Of course. You can be anything you want to be."

Jesse grinned then looked over at Walker quickly. "Cool. Because Uncle Walker said if you could do it, anyone can."

Quinn growled, gripped his son around the stomach. "I think it's time for you to learn what happens when you listen to Uncle Walker. It's the tickle monster!"

Jesse giggled and tried to get away, but Quinn didn't relent, tickling his son until they were both laughing and out of breath on the floor.

"No mercy!"

"Please, Daddy!"

"Tell me I'm the master of the universe!"

"You're the master of the universe!"

"Tell me Uncle Walker stinks!"

"Uncle Walker stinks!"

Quinn grinned over his shoulder at Walker, then patted his son's stomach. "You were saved. But remember, I am always watching."

Jesse yawned and Quinn shook his head to clear his thoughts. Already the new council and one of its members were distracting him from what was really important in his life. Yes, the Pack and the danger from within and what seemed to be coming was number two on his priorities. His son was number one.

Gideon knew about the broken mate bond and had given Quinn leeway when it came to Pack responsibilities.

Quinn was one of Gideon's lieutenants, in essence, a bodyguard. He would willingly lay down his life to save his Alpha's. Though that would leave Jesse alone without him, he knew the Brentwoods would take him in as one of their own.

The parallel to Gina's own history was not lost on him.

That didn't mean he'd listen to those thoughts.

Instead, he pushed them aside and picked up his son. Jesse mumbled something intelligible in his ear then fell asleep on his shoulder. Quinn sighed, gave Walker a look, and then went to go tuck his son in.

It wasn't even dark yet and Jesse was asleep. Quinn knew Jess was deteriorating, but it was as though Jesse—and Quinn for that matter—were trapped in quicksand. No matter what he did, nothing helped. Whenever he tried to find a way to help his son, he and Walker ended up in pain, and his son was no better.

There had to be a way to keep Jesse from fading away, but Quinn didn't know what it was.

Maybe, just maybe, if they found favor with the moon goddess again, she'd save his son.

He didn't hold out much hope for that, though. He'd given up on fate long ago, but if it meant that his son would live a healthy life, he'd do everything in his power to make that happen.

He tucked Jesse in then went back into the kitchen where Walker sat with two beers. Though they were wolves and their metabolism burned through alcohol quickly, it was the symbol that mattered. Plus, he just liked the taste.

Walker sipped his beer and studied him. Quinn just sighed and let it happen. The other wolf always seemed to do that. He was a thoughtful Healer who used his quiet nature to put his patients at ease, unlike the Redwood Healer, Hannah, the witch who used her smiles and soft words to help her den. Quinn had only met the woman a few times over the years, but he'd had no qualms about her or her two mates. They were a true triad, and their bond helped Hannah's Healing.

Walker had only himself, and sometimes Quinn thought the other wolf figured it wasn't enough.

The fact that no one could heal Jesse made it seem only more evident.

Maybe when Walker took a mate, things would be better.

Just another reason they had to figure out what was wrong with their Pack.

"Gideon is on his way," Walker finally said.

Quinn took a sip of his beer, letting the amber ale settle on his tongue before he swallowed. Right then, if he could find a way to get drunk without drinking a couple of bottles of tequila, he'd eagerly take it.

As it was, he was forced to deal with his warring thoughts and the fact that his Alpha had put such trust in him. He didn't know that he was worthy.

He wasn't the same wolf he'd been before Helena. He was only forty-five, yet he felt so much older.

"Did he tell you about what the meeting covered?" Quinn finally asked. He needed to get his head out of his ass and actually pay attention to the man in front of him, rather than a past he couldn't change.

Walker nodded. "Yes. You're leading a new council." He raised a brow. "Or, rather, co-leading with Gina."

Quinn scowled at the way the other man said her name. As if he knew her more than he should or something.

"How do you know Gina?"

Walker took a sip of his beer, his gaze on Quinn. "She sometimes works with Hannah when she's not working with Adam."

Quinn frowned. "I thought she was going to be the Enforcer. Not the Healer. Why would she need to work with Hannah? And how did I not know you work with Hannah?"

Walker rolled his eyes then put his beer down. "First, I work with Hannah because she's the closest Healer to me. It's nice to have another person who understands the bonds I hold with the Pack. Though her power is different because it comes from her witch blood, rather than being a wolf, it has the same basic premise as mine. As for Gina, she works with Hannah because Hannah is not only family, but a witch."

At Quinn's dumbfounded look, Walker shook his head.

"Gina needs guidance when it comes to her powers. She's only in her twenties, so she has a lot to learn. Hannah had not only her own mother to teach her how to use her powers, but the coven as well before she left years ago. Years before she even met the Redwoods and her mates. Gina doesn't have a mother who can show her the ropes. I believe Gina's mother, Larissa, was just beginning to get to the baser parts of their magic when she and her mate, Neil, were killed." Walker sighed. "Melanie might be a strong and powerful Alpha female and a fantastic mother, but she is not a witch. She can't show Gina what she needs because it's not inherent to her. So Hannah helps."

"That's nice of her," Quinn mumbled.

Walker snorted. "The whole Jamenson family works as a unit. I mean, all of them are mated, and most of them have two or three children. Kade and Melanie have seven kids, just like Kade's parents had. They're a huge family. They might be around our age, but they're further along than the Brentwoods when it comes to matings and procreating."

Quinn sighed. "Well, they also had a previous Alpha pair who knew what the hell they were doing. Edward and Patricia were wolves of legend." He shook his head. "Our previous Alpha? Not so much."

The fact that Quinn was talking about Walker's father was not lost on him. Then again, there was no love lost with that family tale and the history of the Talons.

Walter just lifted a brow then picked up his beer for another drink.

Quinn looked over when he scented his Alpha and Beta at the door. They didn't bother to knock since he hadn't locked the door behind him. Plus, they were always welcome in his home because they helped protect his son.

"I see you've started on the drinking without us," Gideon said, his voice tired. Quinn didn't know what it felt like to be Alpha, but he knew he'd never want the weight of that responsibility on his shoulders.

Mitchell scowled then went to the fridge, pulling out a couple of beers. Mitchell was a pain in the ass, but considering what the man had gone through, Quinn didn't blame him one bit.

"So, a council," Quinn said once they were all seated and drinking. "Why didn't you warn me?"

Gideon merely gave him a look. "Since when have I had to explain any decisions I've made when it comes to this Pack?"

Quinn lowered his eyes. "I meant no disrespect," he said, his voice a growl.

Gideon just sighed. "Stop it. I didn't tell you because Kade wasn't going to tell Gina or the others we wanted on the council. And yes, Kade and I knew who we wanted on our councils before we showed up for the meeting, but we didn't tell each other. We wanted to wait until we were there for the reveal or what have you. Only Mitchell and Jasper knew what was going on, but not to the full extent. Not even our Enforcers or Heirs knew because we wanted to keep things equal and not let politics get in the way. Though, with any Pack melding, there's going to be politics." His Alpha snarled the last part, and Quinn felt better.

At least he wasn't the only one kept in the dark. "So you didn't tell Ryder about it because he's the Heir just like Finn? Finn's a bit young to be part of all of this." Finn was Kade's oldest son, and therefore the Redwood Pack Heir. He'd also been forced to hold that mantel since he was just a little boy of three. Not only had Finn almost been killed the year before *that* in the war, he then had to deal with the new powers flowing through his veins when the former Alpha, his grandfather, had died at the hands of the demon.

It had been a dark time for all werewolves that day.

Gideon scratched his chin. "Pretty much. Though the boy is an adult now by human standards, so Kade is going to start giving him more responsibility, I think. The kid's not that hotheaded. Not like we were when we were his age. The fact that he had every bone in his body broken when he was two, thanks to the demon, changed him. War and loss changes you. Paves your path in a different direction when you're not looking."

He winced at the reminder of Finn's injuries. The kid was okay now, but that couldn't have been an easy experience. "So now we all know?" Quinn asked, taking a sip of his beer.

"Yes. We're not going to keep it a secret. This council isn't for backdoor dealings or political maneuvers. It's about a way to make sure our future actually arrives. I'm afraid if we don't start working together for more than just a few days a year, we're going to fuck it up when something changes."

Quinn tilted his head. "What changes?"

His Alpha shook his head. "I don't know. Something's coming, and we need to find a way to grow before it happens." He met Quinn's eyes. "Are you going to be able to work with Gina? We still have time to shift things if you're having issues. Issues you can't overcome, that is."

It was a challenge, and everyone in the room knew it. If Quinn said he wanted out, he'd look weak to the rest of the Pack, as well as the Redwoods. So it didn't matter that he wouldn't back out anyway; he now had no choice.

He didn't like being moved like a chess piece, but sometimes an Alpha had no choice.

Gideon might be a young Alpha, as young in terms of experiences as Kade, but he was not a cruel Alpha. If he didn't think Quinn could handle it, he wouldn't have given the task to him in the first place.

Quinn just had to believe it.

"I can handle it," Quinn growled. He took a deep breath, calming himself. "I can handle it." He sounded better that time.

Gideon gave him an assessing look then nodded. "Good. Gina should be talking with Kade now about the next meeting. From now on, you two will plan the places and times, but for this first one, the Alphas did it for you. So tomorrow at ten a.m. in the place we met before. Got it?"

Quinn nodded.

"Good. She should be calling you soon to confirm." Gideon drained his beer then stood up. "So don't fuck it up by ignoring her."

Quinn snarled.

"I heard you, Quinn. Just don't fuck it up."

With that, the Brentwoods left his home, and Quinn stood there, shaking his head. He hated when things were out of control. His life, his work, his son, his wolf…and now he was at it again. He knew his Pack needed him to be strong, needed him to work with the Redwoods since that was the whole point of the council, but that didn't make it easy.

His phone beeped, and he answered, already knowing who it would be.

"Quinn here."

"Quinn, it's Gina."

Her voice slid through him and went straight to his cock. He held back a growl and forced himself to ignore his reaction.

"Gideon told me the time and place." He didn't know why he couldn't just stay calm and not antagonize, but he couldn't bear to listen to her. She stirred up too many things for him.

And she was a goddamn witch.

She paused. "Fine," she clipped. "See you then. I was just calling to confirm."

"Consider it confirmed." He hung up and threw his phone on the couch.

If he didn't think about her too much, didn't worry about that annoying ache in his wolf, he'd be fine. Once he pushed her away and set the boundaries, they'd all be able to act normally.

Or as normal as a wolf with only half a soul could act.

Chapter Three

That insufferable brute needed a swift kick in the ass.

Sure, he had sexy eyes and even sexier ink on thick muscles, but damn it.

Gina's thoughts had been on a loop with that and a few other choice words since the bastard had hung up on her the day before.

She scrunched her face and forced herself to calm down. The dirt beneath her feet clouded around her, and she paused in her pacing. She was only making a mess of herself and not helping anything.

She didn't need to go into the meeting looking as though she wanted to rip out his throat.

That probably wouldn't be good for the whole treaty thing.

But goddess, she wanted to hurt him, mess up his pretty face. No, that wasn't right. He wasn't pretty. His face held too many hard edges for that. But his brutal handsomeness called to her wolf, and she hated the fact that it did.

And now, she couldn't get his face out of her head.

This didn't bode well for the meeting with the other wolves. It was going to take everything in her power not to reveal her thoughts to the rest of them. Especially Parker. Her cousin saw too much within others. That was probably why he was so good at what he did. Ever since he was a kid, he could break up altercations with his words; he never needed his fists. He'd gained dominance in the Pack because of it, though he could fight when needed. He was also one hell of a dominant wolf, which made him a double threat. That was why he'd been chosen to be part of the council in the first place.

She would just have to make sure she didn't react to Quinn like her wolf wanted to.

Easier said than done.

"What are you thinking about so hard?" Parker asked as he came up to her side.

Gina looked over at her cousin and smiled. He was taller than her by at least half a foot, and he had grown wider in the past couple of years as he bulked up. He wasn't the young kid she'd met when she'd joined the family. Then again, she wasn't a kid either.

Of course, Parker's unruly hair was the same. His light brown hair went in every direction possible but still looked as though he'd paid for it to be that way. The ladies of the Pack seemed to love it.

Between him and Finn, the younger Jamenson men were proving to be every bit as lethal as their fathers. The other kids, all of Gina's brothers and cousins, were showing that same edge.

Of course, all the girl cousins were so different that she wasn't sure they'd ever match their famous aunt Cailin's attitude and rebellious streak, but a few of them were trying.

Gina was one of them, but that was only by accident.

She couldn't help the fact she was a dominant wolf.

"Gina?"

She shook her head and leaned into Parker. He put his arm around her shoulder, and she sighed. "Just thinking about how old we're all getting."

Parker snorted. "Well, we're not *that* old, but I, for one, am glad that we're getting an adult job right now. You know? We aren't kids anymore."

"No. We aren't."

They were the next generation of wolves. Scary to think that her younger siblings and cousins would one day help rule the Redwoods.

"I'm here. Let's go."

Gina turned around at Farah's voice. She didn't know the other woman well but knew Farah was older than both she and Parker by a couple decades. Her dark hair fell to her butt while braided, and her large, dark eyes gave her a youthful look.

Farah was quiet, but when she spoke, her voice held impatience. She wasn't as dominant as Gina or Parker, and that fact apparently didn't sit well with her from the look on her face.

Well, that wasn't Gina's problem as long as Farah didn't try any dominance games. After all, they were here to form an alliance and council with the Talons, not show weakness.

"We're ready," Gina said, her voice holding her wolf in check since she couldn't let the other woman think she was more dominant. They were wolves, not humans.

They were only a five-minute run or fast walk from the meeting place. They'd each driven to the Redwood meeting place separately since they had other things to do that morning, but now they could walk to the Talons as a unit. She was pretty sure Quinn would be doing the same. There were just some things that needed to be done as a show of Pack unity, even though both Packs were supposed to be friendly.

When they made it to the meeting place in the middle of neutral territory, Gina had to hold back a smile at the sight of the three Talon members. They were walking into the area in the exact same fashion as the Redwoods. At least they were on the same page in that respect. Hopefully that boded well for the others.

"Quinn," she said, her voice neutral. He stared at her with such intensity it took everything in her power not to either bow her head or rub up on him. Neither would be appropriate.

Her wolf whimpered.

Damn wolf.

"Gina." His voice hit her in all the right places, and she held back a curse.

This was going to be a freaking long day.

"This is Parker and Farah." She nodded toward her Packmates, who said their hellos.

"And this is Lorenzo and Kimberly," Quinn said, his voice so deep she wasn't sure it wasn't a growl.

After the introductions, they made their way into the meeting room. It was a little awkward since no one spoke, but today would be a day of testing ground, rather than making major decisions. This wasn't a competition but a way to make things work in the long run.

She just hoped no blood would be spilled.

Quinn might be the most dominant wolf in the room, but Parker—and even she—weren't far behind. In fact, now that she thought about it, she wasn't sure who would win between Quinn and Parker. Parker always seemed to surprise those who fought him.

Okay, enough of letting her mind wander.

"Where should we begin?" she asked, trying to get things started to deflect Quinn's gaze.

Kimberly, a quiet wolf who was clearly one of the maternal wolves from the way her wolf radiated that power, tilted her head. "I'm not sure what we're supposed to do here. It's all a little vague."

Farah snorted beside Gina, and she held back a growl at the other woman's attitude.

"It's supposed to be vague," Parker said, his voice calm, not reacting to Farah or the other dominant wolves in the room. "We need to figure out how to help the Packs. If they knew exactly what to do, then we wouldn't be needed."

"True," Lorenzo put in. The dark wolf was seriously built and looked as though he could take down a whole den with just one fist. Though his power didn't seem on the level of Quinn's, he was still a powerful wolf in the grand scheme of things.

"We should toss out ideas on how to improve the way the Packs work together," Quinn said.

Gina nodded. His thoughts were on the same page as hers. "Right. Then we can evaluate them and decide which one or ones to try once we have a plan. It doesn't have to be something drastic. Even the little things matter."

Quinn rubbed his jaw, and Gina had to keep her eyes from his. If she met his gaze, then he'd see her want, her need. That wasn't something she could allow.

"So, what do you have?" she asked. Her voice was calm, despite the war inside her.

They started tossing out ideas that included such things as forcing people to come together for a purpose or opening the wards and having day visits rather than only necessary ones.

"We could have a set of games," Lorenzo added. "Like Wolf Games."

Gina nodded, writing that one down. "I like that idea. Have people work together and then against one another but in a spirit of competition rather than dominance. Though I think that might be something we do later, when we're a little closer to having the trust we need. You know?"

Lorenzo gave her a small smile, and she smiled back. He might look as though he could kill with a single look, but that smile softened his face dramatically.

Quinn let out a growl, and she frowned at him. What was his problem?

She narrowed her eyes at the sexy wolf then sighed, knowing she was being petty. "We could pair up people on perimeter runs," she put in.

"That's a good idea," Parker said, his voice soft. "We've always protected our own perimeter, but if we put a member from each Pack in a unit, it might help promote friendliness."

"That's putting a lot of trust on the other person," Kimberly said then held up her hand. "I'm not saying it's a bad thing considering that's why we're here, but it's a huge step."

"For it to work, it would have to start with people we know inside and out," Quinn put in.

Gina nodded. "I know. I'm not saying we put two wolves that we don't know well together. But the Alphas want us to work together as a team, so putting those wolves together as a unit would be one step."

"Maybe," Quinn said.

For the love of the goddess, this man was infuriating, but she let it roll off her shoulders. Today was just an idea session. They weren't making any decisions.

"Okay, what about the maternal wolves?" Gina asked.

Kimberly sat up, her eyes narrowed. "What about us?"

Gina smiled. "You guys are the heart of the Pack. You're the ones who help raise our children. You run the schools and keep an eye on even the smallest den member. If we have *them* work together, it could be working from the ground up."

"I don't know that I'd like my children in the other den if I'm not there," Farah said.

Quinn glanced over at Farah then turned back to Gina.

"I don't know if I'd like that either," Lorenzo said softly.

She hadn't known Farah or Lorenzo were parents, but that just made their concerns hold more weight in this area.

Gina shook her head. "I'm not saying we send babies to other dens when you're not there. I'm saying the maternals plan things *together* and get to know one another first. Then as things progress, we teach our children that it's okay to be friends with another Pack. If we start young, they won't learn the prejudices we have now."

Quinn studied her face then gave her a slight nod. "That idea holds merit."

From anyone else, she would have snorted, but with Quinn, that was almost praise.

They talked for another hour, and before she knew it, it was time to call it a day. Quinn met her eyes with a question in his gaze, and she nodded. He was on the same page.

"Time to call it," he said.

"Yep," Gina agreed. "We have good ideas down. I think we should mull them over and each of us work on a plan. Then we can come together again and talk through it. Once we're ready, we can go to the Alphas with our ideas. This way it's not a jumble."

"I agree," Quinn said.

Wow, she was on a roll.

They all stood and began to leave. She let the others leave before her so she could have a moment with Quinn. She knew it was stupid to do so, but if she didn't, her wolf wasn't going to leave her alone.

"What?" he clipped.

She held back an eye roll. "I just wanted to say thank you for listening to my ideas rather than barking at me like last time."

Tact—she had it.

Quinn narrowed his eyes. "I won't let anything harm my Pack or Alpha. If that means I must work with you, witch, then I will."

With that, he stormed away, and she was left frozen.

Witch?

He'd called her a witch.

Why did it sound like a curse on his tongue, rather than just a title?

She swallowed hard and pushed down any feelings she could have had for him. She didn't even know the man. He couldn't hurt her if she didn't let him.

Knowing it would be too much if she didn't release it, she jogged out of the room and into the forest. She felt Parker's eyes on her, but her cousin seemed to know she needed time alone.

She made it to her car, her hands still shaking, and then drove directly to the den and to her home. Her mind warred with itself as she tried to push Quinn's words from her thoughts. The fact that he seemed to hate her just because of who she was, without even knowing her, hurt far more than it should have.

She still lived with her parents even though she was well past the age of moving out. Her brothers were all so much younger that she hadn't wanted to leave her mom alone with them. With six brothers, things could get a bit crazy.

She honestly had no idea how her mom had done it, but now everyone was growing up, and it might be time for her to move out.

Especially now that she had new responsibilities…and her wolf wanted a certain wolf she shouldn't.

When she walked into her home she smiled at her mom, Melanie, talking with Gina's cousin, Brie, and Brie's mother, Willow.

While the men of the family were some of the most dominant wolves in existence, it was a well-known fact that the women of the Jamenson family were the heart and soul.

Plus they could fight to protect what was theirs better than most wolves *because* they held that power.

She might have come into the family through the most painful way possible, by losing her birth parents, but she'd never known a life without love or protection. For that, she was grateful. Even on days where she could barely breathe over the pain of her loss, she knew she had others to lean on when she couldn't do it on her own.

Mel turned to her and smiled. "You're home. We were just talking about you."

Gina raised a brow, and Brie snorted. "Oh really? Should I be scared?"

Willow smiled and squeezed Brie to her side. Willow was in her forties now, but looked to be in her twenties. That's what happened when you were a wolf; genetics favored you. Soon all of the Jamensons would look the same age. The poor humans wouldn't know what hit them.

"We were just talking about roommates," Willow said softly. She wasn't a submissive wolf, but she also wasn't a true dominant. Her aunt fell in that middle territory like so many other wolves, but she still held the same authority as her mate, Jasper.

"Roommates?" Gina asked, then hugged her mom.

Mel kissed her temple, keeping her arm around Gina's waist. Though Gina had been on the verge of needing to shift after her talk with Quinn, just the fact that her mom was there now made things better.

This was what she needed.

"Well, Brie is almost ready to move out," Willow said, her voice a little sad. "I still can't believe my baby is getting older."

"Mom," Brie mumbled, then rolled her eyes.

"What? Your sisters are still young enough that I have a few more years, but the whole leaving-the-nest thing is starting."

"So why were you talking about me?" Gina asked, trying to help alleviate Brie's embarrassment. Brie was a true submissive wolf, which had surprised the family. She wasn't weak by far, but she did need to be loved and protected by dominants. In turn, she'd care for and protect the heart and soul of the dominant. A Pack needed both types of wolves, and Brie, former tomboy and Beta's daughter, fit her role perfectly.

"We were thinking that if and when you move out, you and Brie could be roommates," Mel said.

Gina smiled at the idea. "Oh, I could totally live with that. I was just thinking that it might be time to move out, and yet I didn't want to be alone."

Brie smiled full-out. "Oh, thank the goddess. I was worried you might not want to deal with me."

Gina snorted. "As long as you don't leave your socks and underwear around like Finn and the other boys do, I'm happy."

Brie snapped her fingers. "Darn it. So close!"

Gina laughed then took Brie off to the side to talk places and timing. It would be at least a year until Brie was ready to move out, even though they were talking about it now. Gina could at least move out first and get the lay of the land. Mel and Willow would be there if they needed them, but everyone seemed to know that this was something the girls needed to do on their own.

"Who is that?" Brie asked after they planned a bit.

Gina looked out the window and frowned. "Who is who?"

"That gorgeous wolf with the hot ass. Who is he?"

Gina goggled. "Uh, honey, that is Gideon, the Alpha of the Talon Pack. And you're seventeen. Stop staring."

Brie met her gaze with wide eyes. "I didn't know the Alpha looked like *that*. He never comes around here, so I've never met him."

Considering Gideon usually made Mitchell or Ryder come into the den so they didn't worry any of the wolves, that sort of made sense. Gideon, when he was around, usually came to only the Alpha's house. Right then, he was just leaving the old studio her dad had in the back for when he was drawing.

Gina closed her eyes and prayed that Willow and Mel were busy enough they didn't hear that. "Well forget what's going on in your head. He's the Alpha of the other Pack. You're a teenager. Stop thinking his ass is hot."

Brie just smiled. "I can think it. That doesn't mean I'll act on it. I'm a submissive. He's an Alpha. Those two don't mix. Besides, I think Dad and the uncles might kill me."

"Or him," Gina mumbled. That was so not something she wanted to think about. Considering she was on the council to promote peace and unity between the two Packs, something like that just might make her want to jump out of the nearest window. Again.

They went to find their moms then talked for a bit before Brie and Willow headed out. As soon as they were gone, Mel rubbed the spot between Gina's brows.

"Okay, spill it, baby. What's going on inside that head of yours?"

Gina blinked back tears and shook her head. She wasn't as dominant as her mother and knew if her mom pushed the issue she'd have to tell, but she didn't want to.

"Gina."

With that one word, Gina's shoulders fell, and she told her mom all about the meetings and the dark-eyed wolf she couldn't get out of her head.

Melanie nodded along then sighed. "Oh, baby. While I want to kick that wolf's ass for his tone, you know what this means, don't you?"

She shook her head. "That I should kick his ass on my own?"

Her mom grinned. "Maybe that as well, but, honey, Quinn is your mate."

Gina froze. The thought hadn't even occurred to her.

She'd never felt like this before with another wolf, but this feeling wasn't love or happiness. No, this was all frustration mixed with need and desire. It was only a craving. Quinn couldn't be her mate. They didn't even like each other. Plus, there hadn't been mating between the Redwoods and the Talons yet. This trick of fate wasn't possible.

It couldn't be.

"Gina. Breathe."

She hadn't even realized she was hyperventilating and going lightheaded until Mel took her hand and forced her to sit on the couch.

"I…this can't be happening, Mom." She knew her voice came out as a whine, but she couldn't help it.

"He's a potential from the way your wolf is reacting, sweetie."

She nodded, numb. "A potential doesn't mean I have to do anything about it," she whispered.

"Gina."

At the snap of Melanie's voice, Gina looked over, her brain finally starting to work.

"You know the story of how your father and I met?"

She nodded. It was one of legend, even though it wasn't all honey and roses.

"Kade had a potential mate before me. All wolves have more than one mate out there, though usually there are decades in between meetings, not a few months or days. Fate *does* give us a choice, though usually, we want the wolf meant for us in the first place. The woman your father could have mated had more than one potential at the same time. Kade's friend was the one that other woman chose. Then Kade met me."

Gina nodded, knowing where the story was going.

"I was so scared, Gina. So freaking scared that werewolves were real that I almost missed out on the best things in my life. Yeah, the things that went bump in the night were real, but I should have thought about it more than trying to run. I ran away from him and then met that asshole who thought he could be my mate as well. The fact that I had *two* wolves fighting for me scared me so much I couldn't just come out and say what was in my heart—that I wanted Kade."

"And because we wolves are so bent on rules and tradition, Dad had to fight in a mating circle for you." She knew the story and hated this part as much as Mel did.

Mel growled. "I still think it's a barbaric custom, and when North had to fight Corbin in one later for Lexi? I wanted to find a way out of it, but those damn things are still there because it's *tradition*. If we break one tradition, those wolves not happy with the hierarchy can try to break more, and then things can go bad. Really bad."

Gina nodded then leaned into her mom.

"What I was saying before I went on my diatribe was that I got scared and ran away. I didn't make a decision when I should have, and people got hurt because of it. It has taken many years for me to get over that, and some days I still feel like I need to prove to Kade that I was worth it."

Gina turned and kissed her mom's temple. "You're worth it, and Dad knows it."

Mel gave her a small smile. "Thank you, baby. And about Quinn? You can't know how he will react until you face it. I'm not saying you should mate with him or even tell him. He will be feeling it too, so that decision might be out of your hands. I will say that my running away from your father was the worst decision I've ever made. If it wasn't for your mother, Larissa, pushing me into thinking, I don't know what I would have done."

Gina's eyes watered at the memory. It hurt sometimes to hear Mel talk of Larissa since both women had raised her. She had two mothers who loved her with every ounce of their being. She counted herself lucky.

"I don't know what I'm going to do."

Mel nodded. "You don't have to decide right now." She hugged her hard. "No matter what happens, we're on your side, your Dad and I. I won't tell him or your brothers anything though. I don't want them to interfere."

Gina sighed. "God, they're going to freak out if I mate with Quinn because that's what overbearing male family members do. And if I don't? They're going to freak out even more and kill him or something."

Mel patted her hand. "This is why we're going to let you handle it without their interference."

She nodded then sat there in silence. She needed to think. This was good for the Redwoods and Talons. She *knew* that. The whole point of the council was to find a way to make the Packs work more closely together. Gideon had said the Talons hadn't had a mating in years, and yet here she was, a potential mate for a Talon.

This could be the answer.

Maybe they were finally goddess-blessed.

She swallowed hard.

But she wasn't a pawn, and this wasn't something to check off a list.

This was a decision about people. People who, frankly, didn't even like each other. Quinn growled at her and treated her as though she was nothing more than a nuisance. If he was even feeling the mating urge, he was clearly fighting it.

What she did know, though, was that she couldn't run and hide from it. She couldn't ignore it. She wasn't like Mel, who was newly introduced to wolves. She'd grown up with them, so she didn't have that excuse.

No, she'd tell Quinn.

Tell him that he could be her mate if they both chose.

She knew he had a problem with her being a witch. He'd cursed her for it just that day. She might not know *why* he hated witches, but she'd find out…or walk away when he rejected her. She couldn't help the blood in her veins, the power in her soul.

Her hands shook, and she clenched them. No matter what he said, she'd do right by herself and tell him that. She didn't know what she wanted to do afterward, but if he knew, if he also knew there was a choice, then it was something.

She just prayed that when she told him he wouldn't break her.

She'd leave herself open, bare to anything his wolf chose, because she knew if she didn't, she'd regret it for the rest of her life.

If he left her bloody and broken…then she'd have to live with it.

Somehow.

Chapter Four

Quinn didn't want to deal with another meeting. He didn't want to have to sit in a room with that wolf and her sweet scent. His wolf practically purred like a goddamn cat when she was around, and that couldn't be allowed to happen. Instead of walking toward the meeting area, he'd rather go for a run and burn through every ounce of adrenaline currently flowing through his veins

That was a better idea than dealing with that blasted hybrid wolf.

He couldn't seem to get her out of his mind or her scent off his skin. He hadn't even touched her like his wolf wanted to, yet he could still sense her. Of all wolves, why did it have to be her? Why did he want *this* one?

He hadn't been with a woman since Helena left. It had been five long years since he'd let himself get close to someone else, and he knew it still wasn't enough time. Helena had broken him, shattered every ounce of the man he'd once been. She'd stripped him of half his soul and broken their bond. When it had first happened, he'd passed out from the agonizing pain. The only reason he'd woken up was because he'd heard Jesse cry for him. His little boy had been only a newborn yet had pulled himself from his own nightmare.

By the time he'd healed what he could within himself, he'd been focused on his son and not on the world around him. Gideon had let him remain in his position, and he'd had to fight off dominance challenges since people thought Helena had also damaged his wolf.

Too bad for them that they were wrong about that.

Helena had only strengthened his wolf. He'd had to keep everything sane and strong so he could survive. He hadn't had the time or inclination to find a female to scratch the itch for him. Yeah, wolves needed touch and to release or they'd bottle up too much aggression, but he'd dealt with that. He had his hand to take care of himself when the need arose, and he could run off the adrenaline if needed.

He'd dealt with it all because he was not given a choice. The only reason he hadn't gone off the deep end was because Jesse needed him.

That little boy had saved his life, yet Quinn couldn't do a thing to save him.

He closed his eyes and cursed. No, he would *not* think like that. Jesse would be fine. Once he grew older, he'd get stronger. That was just what would have to happen because the alternative couldn't be in the realm of possibilities.

"Quinn?"

He stiffened at Gina's voice and fisted his hands. Of all people, it had to be her. Why couldn't anyone else come up on him and pull him out of his funk? No, it had to be the fucking witch. He couldn't trust her or her powers, but his wolf sure as hell wanted to try.

What the hell was wrong with him?

Plus, why hadn't he scented her coming up? Even when he was in his mind, he could *always* feel someone entering his space, yet he hadn't with Gina. His wolf *liked* having her there, so he hadn't warned him. Her scent was already in his pores, so he hadn't noticed it coming back.

What the fuck?

God, he needed his head examined.

"What?" he growled then cursed. His problems with her had to stop. He knew he was being an asshole, but something about her rubbed him the wrong way. If he didn't start acting better, he'd screw up this whole thing with the Talons and Redwoods. Even though, for some reason, she put him on edge, he wasn't going to let his Alpha down because of it.

"Sorry, I was just thinking. What's going on?" he asked. There. That was civil.

She tilted her head and stared at him. There was something different about her today, but he couldn't put his finger on it. He also didn't know why he cared about that. He'd work with her because he had to then go back to the den and ignore her. It was the best way for both of them.

"My Alpha just called. He needs Parker for something right away, so he won't be here, and Farah's son got hurt on the playground because he was trying to climb high in the trees. So it will just be me in the meeting. Do you want to reschedule?"

He narrowed his eyes. "So the Redwoods are getting out of their responsibilities so quickly?"

Gina growled. "Fuck you, Quinn. Parker was needed by his Alpha. That trumps us. And hello...Farah's pup is hurt. That trumps us as well. Get over it. I'm here."

He immediately felt like an ass. "The pup okay?"

Her face softened marginally. "Yes. He broke his arm, so he's going to shift to try to fix it. Hannah will be there just in case. When they're young, they don't like using Healing all the time just in case shifting can help. That way they learn to use their wolf rather than rely on outside sources."

"I know. My son is five, and we try to make him shift when he's hurt." He didn't know why he mentioned Jesse, but it had just slipped out.

Gina looked as though he'd slapped her, and she swayed on her feet. He quickly reached out and gripped her elbow. He sucked in a breath at the heat of her skin. His wolf rubbed along their touch, panting for more.

"What's wrong?"

She shook her head then moved from his touch. His wolf whimpered. "I...I didn't know you were mated."

He frowned at her reaction, but he understood her unasked question. Wolves couldn't have children unless they created a mating bond. Sometimes, if people married and loved each other enough, over time, a bond would form with the humans first and the wolves would eventually follow. That was the only way for them to have children.

"I'm not mated." His words were clipped, and he didn't elaborate.

Confusion covered her face, but she didn't ask why. She'd think that Helena had died, and, in every sense of the word, she had for him. If Gina hadn't heard the story of Helena's betrayal, he wasn't going to enlighten her.

Gina licked her lips then shook her head. "What do you want to do about the meeting?"

Glad she had changed the subject, he took out his phone. "I'll tell Lorenzo and Kimberly not to come. The two of us are early, so they probably haven't left yet."

She nodded but didn't leave his side as he messaged the others.

"When do you want the next meeting?" he asked. He needed to get out of her presence or he'd do something horrific, like let his wolf have what it wanted.

"In a couple days should work, but let me get back to you on that."

He nodded then had started to turn away when she gripped his arm.

He held back his snarl and looked down at her pale hand on his darker skin.

"What?"

"Since we're both here, how about we start on the cooperation for the Pack?"

He frowned and pulled from her touch. "What do you mean?"

She shifted from foot to foot, and he frowned. The two other times he'd met her she'd been self-assured and not so fidgety. Something had happened between the last time and now, but he had no idea what. Nor was he sure he wanted to know in the first place.

"How about you and I go on a perimeter run and then end up at the Talon den?"

He widened his eyes. "Seriously?"

She nodded. "Yes. Those two things were on top of our list to begin with, and since we're the leaders of the council, it makes sense that we'd do a trial run. I'm not saying we become friends and have me stay the night or anything." She blushed, and he blinked. Wherever her thoughts had gone, she hadn't meant for them to.

He knew he should say no and wait to do something along those lines later, but for some reason, he didn't want to. It was a damned good idea, and he had a feeling that if they'd had the meeting today, they'd have ended up doing this exact thing anyway. He and Gina *had* to be the first people to try out cooperating. They were in the leadership roles, and if they couldn't get along with one another, they weren't doing their jobs.

The fact that he knew he'd been an asshole with her didn't sit well with him, but he needed to keep acting like one. If he didn't, he'd let his wolf have control and do something stupid—like pull her closer so he could inhale her sweet scent.

He didn't trust her, he told himself.

She was a witch. Those powers had shattered his soul and had almost killed him and his son. He would never trust her, even if his wolf wanted to—and the Pack needed him to.

Instead of listening to that, though, he nodded. "Fine. We'll run as wolves so we have better senses. You got a problem with that?"

She shook her head. "That's what I wanted to do anyway. I have a backpack my uncle Josh made that fits me in my wolf form. I can get in and out of it without human hands. I'll put our clothes in it. That way we don't have to leave them here to pick up later."

He nodded and held back a frown. He'd wanted them to run as wolves without the preliminaries so he wouldn't have to speak to her and get to know her. He *needed* the space between them. But now he knew he'd see her without her clothes. Probably not the best move for a man who wanted to get a woman out of his head.

He followed her to the side of the building where she'd stashed her bag.

"Strip down and give me your clothes. I'll pack them up and then shift."

He raised a brow at her tone and watched her ears redden. Wolves weren't supposed to care about nudity since they had to shift naked. It was supposed to be casual. They wore clothes inside the den common areas for the children, but usually, they weren't modest.

The fact that the both of them were reacting to each other's presence didn't bode well.

He turned away from her and stripped off his shirt then toed off his shoes. He took a deep breath then shucked off his pants and boxer briefs. He heard the wisp of fabric behind him and knew she was doing the same. His wolf nudged at him, and he held back a curse. The thought of her naked behind him wasn't doing him any favors, and now his cock was hard against his belly.

Shifting with a hard-on was not pleasant.

He sighed then folded his clothes in a pile. Damn it. He wasn't some young pup who had never seen a naked woman before. It shouldn't matter that she wasn't wearing clothes. They were wolves.

He picked up his clothes and turned around.

Dear. Goddess.

She was perfect. All thick curves and muscles mixed into one. Her nipples were dark and erect. Her breasts were larger than his palms although, in clothes, she didn't look as though she had all those curves. Her belly was smooth and looked soft, bitable, and flared out to sexy, grip-worthy hips. He pulled his gaze up to her face before he caught sight of her pussy. Once he did, he knew he'd be in trouble.

He didn't even *like* her, yet his eyes feasted on her.

He handed her his clothes as she kept her wide eyes on his face. He could smell her arousal, taste it on his tongue, and he knew he needed to get out of there fast.

With a grunt, he turned to his side then knelt on all fours. The change from human to wolf and then back was not easy. It took minutes instead of a flash of light and fuzzy feeling, like some would choose to believe. Those minutes dragged on in agony as bones broke, ligaments tore, and fur sprouted from his skin. The stronger the wolf, the shorter time it took to change, but that didn't make it any less painful.

His face elongated, and his body hunched. They weren't the werewolves from the old movies. No, they were true wolves. Some might be slightly bigger than the wild ones humans had almost killed off, but not most.

By the time he finished shifting, he was tired, yet edgy at the same time. He needed a good run and knew that the perimeter check with Gina would get that done. He turned toward Gina and saw she was almost done shifting, her body panting with the exertion. She was even more dominant that he'd thought if she was so close to him in terms of timing.

When she was done, she shook her body then wiggled into her backpack. He couldn't help but notice the grace of her wolf. Strength and a sense of fragility entwined together to make a truly magnificent shifter.

While he was a dark gray wolf with only one white foot, she was chocolate brown with a solid white stripe on her nose. She also kept her blue eyes from her human form, but that solid ring of yellow around her irises told him her wolf was close to the surface.

He gave her a nod then started to turn. They couldn't talk in this form so they had to use body movements to communicate. Gina yipped at him—wolves didn't bark—and he stopped. She came up to him and sniffed around him, sticking her nose along his neck. He stood still, knowing from the look in her eyes before she'd gotten closer that this was her wolf, not her human half, that needed to do this.

She wasn't a submissive wolf, but he was a clear dominant that she'd never seen before in wolf form. Her wolf *needed* some kind of reassurance, whether it be scent or something else, so she could move on.

Quinn might not trust her because of her witch half—and also, if he was honest with himself, because of his attraction to her—but he couldn't let a lower ranked wolf down. He growled softly then nipped at the back of her neck. She let out a sigh then lowered her head.

He let his fangs gently press into her fur then let go. Her wolf met his gaze then did a little nod.

With that over, he turned back toward his den then started off at a run. He heard Gina's paws hit the ground behind him. He wasn't going at full speed, so he knew she could keep up. She was going to be the Enforcer of her Pack, so she wasn't weak or slow.

They kept at it for a good thirty minutes, scenting around the perimeter to ensure there wasn't anything out of place. He watched the way she came up to his side, her nose on the ground when they paused, and the way her ears were always perked, on alert.

She was a good scout, a gorgeous wolf.

Maybe if he could ever learn to trust another person again, he might like her.

That, though, wouldn't be happening.

They made their way back to the edge of the den and stopped. He gave her a look, and if a wolf could roll their eyes and look exasperated, he was pretty sure Gina's wolf did. She wiggled back out of her backpack and unzipped it with her teeth. She'd apparently done this before. He usually just left his clothes wherever he shifted since he shifted in his home or out in the fields for the wolf hunt. If he shifted outside those two places, it was for a reason, and he didn't much care about clothes.

He let his body shift back, wincing at the pain. They'd both need food once they got to his place, or they'd be too tired to walk through the den when they were done. Plus, with her being an outside wolf, he didn't want her weakened in case another wolf had an issue.

His place?

Well, that hadn't been in the cards, but now he didn't know where else to bring her. Hell. So much for avoiding her at all costs.

He shifted back and then pulled on his clothes and shoes without looking at her. He'd already crossed that boundary before and wouldn't be doing it again.

When he felt her come to his side, he looked down at the top of her head. She wasn't short, but since he was so large, she seemed tiny next to him.

"We're going to my place to eat so you can build up your energy. Then you and I can walk around the den and go with the plan."

"Sounds good to me," she said, her voice breathless.

They both needed to get out of there. Fast.

She followed him through the edge of the forest to the den. He cursed when he remembered how she was going to get through the wards.

"Grab my hand," he bit out. "I can get you through the wards since you're invited in with me."

He didn't look at her but sucked in a breath when her soft palm slid into his. His wolf growled and threw his body against him, begging for her. Holy crap, it was only her hand, and yet his wolf was going berserk.

He clenched his jaw then walked through the wards, pulling Gina with him. She sucked in a breath but kept moving. He knew the wards were pushing at her, but not as hard as it would have been if she hadn't been holding on to his hand. The magic had to willingly let an outside wolf or person in. The fact that he was inviting her, even reluctantly, told the wards to let her through.

"Oh boy," she said once they got through. He looked back at her and frowned.

"You okay?" he asked despite himself.

She smiled at him and nodded. "Yep. It's weird to go through wards that aren't part of the Redwoods. It was familiar since I could sense the witch and wolf magic that goes into them, but different enough that it was kind of a thrill."

At the word *witch*, he shut down. He pulled his hand away and turned toward his home. He shouldn't have brought her here. He shouldn't have led her to his home. She should be back in her precious den with her witch powers and away from him.

Instead, he was bringing the beast into his den.

What the hell had he been thinking?

He heard her scurry behind him, but he kept going, ignoring the looks of his fellow Packmates. Some growled at her; others nodded and waved. It was to be expected. The Packs had been as friendly as they were for fifteen years. Some had probably met Gina before. Others wouldn't know who she was but saw a wolf they didn't know in their den. The fact that she was with Quinn didn't matter when he wasn't actually near enough to her to show that he could protect her and the den.

He knew he was screwing this up, but he'd deal with it after he ate.

He walked up to his door and cursed.

"Jesse," he whispered as his son opened the door.

"Dad! You're home."

Quinn leaned down and picked up his little boy, inhaling his soft scent. "What are you doing here, Jesse?"

Walker came out from behind him, his brows raised. "Jesse had a tough day at school so he wanted to nap here instead of at Ryder's place. Since I was around, I stayed so Ryder could get some work done. You going to get out of the way so Gina can come inside?"

"Gina?" Jesse asked and looked over Quinn's shoulder fully. "Hi. I'm Jesse." The little boy smiled, and Quinn wanted to growl and hide his son. He knew it made no sense.

He *knew* Gina wasn't the witch that hurt his son.

He just couldn't get that prejudice out of his head.

He was a goddamn bastard.

Quinn set Jesse down then moved out of the way so Gina could walk in. "Jesse, this is Gina. She's a Redwood who's working with me."

Gina got down at Jesse's level so they were eye to eye. "Hi, Jesse. It's nice to meet you."

Jesse grinned and leaned into Quinn's leg. "Hi. You're pretty."

Quinn closed his eyes and held back a groan. Like father, like son. Though from the way Gina had smiled at his son, Jesse was doing better than him.

Not that Quinn wanted to do any better. Nope. He was going to feed her then do his job so he could get her out of there. He opened his eyes and stared at the two of them, knowing he probably should split them up before something happened.

"Thank you, Jesse. You're handsome, yourself."

Jesse smiled big and leaned toward Gina. "Daddy says he's the master of the universe. Are you the master too since you're on the council?"

Gina blinked, then raised her brow at Quinn.

Quinn did his best not to shuffle his feet like some teenage pup.

"He says he's the master of the universe?" she asked, laughter in her voice.

Jesse nodded. "Uh huh. I have to say it or he won't quit tickling me."

Gina snorted then. "I see. So that means you only say it under duress."

Jesse's eyes widened and then he shook his head. "But he *is* the master of the universe."

"Sure, honey. I believe you."

"You should. I know things."

"Really? So, how old are you that you know so many things?"

Gina stood but leaned against the couch so Jesse could feel better. She put herself out of an aggressive position so the pup would feel safe. Clearly she'd been around kids before.

"I'm five." Jesse yawned.

"Five? Already? You're growing up fast."

Quinn swallowed hard at the reminder and cleared his throat. "Okay, buddy, you need to get some sleep if you're yawning."

Gina frowned and looked outside at the sun in the sky. She didn't understand, and Quinn wasn't sure he wanted to enlighten her.

"I can put Jesse to bed," Walker said, his voice soft. "Good to see you, Gina. I figure you and Quinn here are ready to get some food and be on your way. I know what you're trying to accomplish, and I think it will do some good."

He said his good-byes, and Quinn hugged his son. Jesse even hugged Gina before heading back to his room. Jesse didn't have many females in his life—only Gideon's sister, Brynn, really—so it was odd to see him attach himself to Gina so quickly.

"Food?" Quinn asked, knowing he sounded like an idiot.

Gina gave him an odd look then nodded. "Okay. Then we walk around the den like idiots and try to show people that we're friends?"

Quinn turned and frowned. "Excuse me?"

Gina gave him a sad smile. "I know you don't want me here. I know you didn't want to touch my hand to get me through the wards. Hell, Quinn, you even stiffened when Jesse came by. I mean, did you really think I was going to hurt your son? I don't know why you hated me on sight, but there's something we need to talk about."

He growled, wanting her out of his house, away from him before he did something stupid, like apologize.

"There's nothing we need to talk about."

"Yes, yes there is, you idiot."

"Get out, Gina. We can do this another time. Or better yet, you and Lorenzo can."

She shook her head. "You feel it, don't you?"

"Feel what?" He ran a hand over his head and clenched his jaw. When he met her gaze, the tears in them surprised him.

"We're mates, Quinn."

He let out a breath and took a step back. His head whirled, and he tried to swallow. "What?"

No. Hell no. This couldn't be happening.

She shook her head, a single tear sliding down her cheek. She gave a small laugh, only it sounded hollow.

"Maybe you didn't know. My wolf though? She wants you as her own. I know the Talons and Redwoods haven't mated since the treaty, but apparently fate changed her mind."

He didn't know what to say. What to think. What the hell? He wasn't supposed to have another mate. He'd already *had* a mate. One that left him, broke him, and almost killed him and his son.

Instead of thinking, he said the first thing that came to mind.

"Fuck fate."

Her eyes widened, and she took a step back as though he'd slapped her. "Fuck fate?" she whispered.

"Fuck it. You don't get it, Gina. I don't care what fate says because I'm not mating again. I already had one. I'm not doing it again."

Tears filled her eyes, but she nodded. "I...I get it. When my uncle Adam lost his mate, he refused to mate Bay. It was only an accident they were mated in the first place."

He shook his head. "I'm not like your uncle Adam. His mate died. I know the story. My mate? She's alive, Gina."

She scrunched her face. "How can that be?"

He let out a hollow laugh. "How? Because that stupid bitch went to a goddamn *witch* and broke our mating bond. She also almost killed our son in the process."

"Oh, Quinn, I'm so sorry." Tears were flowing freely now, but he ignored them.

"Jesse is hanging by a thread, and there's nothing I can do about it. You think I want another mate when I already had my chance? I lost it because she found greener pastures or some shit. She chose that life over what she had and broke my soul. I don't want another freaking mate, let alone a witch I will never trust."

She froze, her face going deathly pale.

"So go and find yourself another mate if that's what you want. You know you'll find another since apparently fate is a fickle bitch. But I don't want a mate. Not now. And if I did, it wouldn't be you, a witch. A witch was the reason my bond was broken, and I could never trust you. You're the epitome of everything I hate."

As soon as he said it, he wanted to take it back.

He didn't hate Gina.

He hated the women who had hurt him.

Yet he'd put five years of hate in those words, and now he had to deal with the look on her face.

"Gina…"

She held up her hand. "You said enough." Her voice was low, devoid of any emotion. Her cheeks were dry but red. "I'm going to leave. I can get out of the wards through the front entrance without having an anchor. The guards there know I'm here by now and will know that I'm leaving. I'll see you at the next meeting."

She turned then froze. "I never said I wanted to be your mate, Quinn. I only said that there was the potential. I'm sorry those women hurt you. I'm not them, but you'll never believe that." She took a shaky breath, and Quinn wanted to hold her and tell her he was sorry.

He knew if he did that he'd never stop, and she had to get out of his house. If she stayed, he didn't know what he'd do.

"I hope your little boy is okay. You should call Hannah to see if she can help."

With that, she left, and he stood there, his head lowered.

"Jesus fucking Christ, Quinn," Walker growled. "First, you're lucky

Jesse is out cold. Second? I didn't know you were so cruel. You broke her."

Quinn had forgotten Walker was there but didn't turn to face the other man.

"Just go," he whispered.

"I knew Helena scarred you, but shit, Quinn, you can't let her ruin your future."

Quinn growled and let his power roll through the room. Walker didn't bow. Instead, the Healer pushed his own power back.

Quinn staggered and lowered his head.

"Yeah, I'm higher ranking than you. Get over it, asshole," Walker cursed. "If Kade ever finds out what you said to her, he'll kill you, and we'll end up in another war. That's politics and family." He sighed. "You're my friend, Quinn, but the man I just saw isn't the man I know, the man I'm friends with. That man is not Jesse's father. Remember that."

Walker stormed out of the house, and Quinn sank to the floor, his head in his hands. Walker was right. He *had* been an asshole to Gina. He hadn't meant to lash out like he had, and now he'd hurt her more than he'd ever meant to.

The only thing he knew was that he hadn't deserved Helena, and he damn well didn't deserve Gina. She'd find another wolf to mate and find her happiness.

She wasn't for Quinn.

He wasn't for her.

He didn't deserve anything.

Chapter Five

The ground beneath her feet gave way, and Gina fell on her knees. Rocks and twigs dug into her skin, and dirt covered her palms as she knelt on all fours, determined not to break.

Though hadn't she already broken?

Her limbs ached, but not as much as her heart.

She'd made it to the den, through the wards, and couldn't keep going.

She didn't even *like* Quinn, yet he'd hurt her in a way she never thought possible.

She'd known he might not want to mate with her. That was to be expected. They didn't know each other that well and hadn't gotten off on the right foot. It wasn't as though she was expecting a mating mark and for him to jump her right there.

Even she hadn't been ready for that.

But she'd thought he might actually talk to her about it.

God, how wrong she'd been.

She licked her lips and forced herself to sit down rather than kneel. He'd had a mate; she'd known that. After all, how else would he have Jesse?

She'd assumed that Jesse's mother had died though. Wolves were not like humans. They couldn't cheat on each other. What would be the point? Their bodies didn't want another and their hearts sure as hell didn't. Their souls were eternally entwined once both parts of the mating were locked into place.

Or, at least, that's how it was supposed to be.

Once that happened, wolves couldn't feel other potentials out in the world. That would be irrevocably cruel. Fate might be a tricky bitch, but she wasn't cruel.

Well, maybe she was.

When she'd figured out the tug and pull she felt with Quinn was the mating urge, she'd thought his mate was dead. That had to have been the only way for her to feel that energy.

She'd known it wouldn't be easy. She'd heard stories of her uncle Adam and the pain he'd felt and caused because of his first mate, Anna. When she'd been killed, he'd put up a stone wall between him and the world. When Bay had come into his life and torn down that wall, it hadn't been a road paved with flowers.

Gina had expected a rough road. She'd expected that Quinn might not want her at all. After all, she wasn't sure she wanted him either, but she'd put herself on the line because she'd needed to be honest with herself.

What she hadn't expected was the hate.

Oh, goddess, the hate.

He'd looked at her as though she'd shown him the end of the world, as if she was *nothing*.

He didn't want her.

She got that.

She'd known that was a possibility.

The fact that he'd pushed her away not only because he didn't want her, but because of what she was—a witch—hurt more than she could bear.

The epitome of everything I hate.

She choked back a sob.

How was she supposed to face him at the council meetings? How was she supposed to protect her Pack's future when the one wolf her wolf ached for hated her?

It wasn't supposed to hurt this much.

She rubbed the spot between her breasts and tried to catch her breath. Tears slid down her cheeks, and her body shook. She sniffed, trying to control it, and then just let herself go. She threw her head back and howled, her voice holding the song of her heart...or what was left of it.

The sound of someone running up behind her filled her ears, but she didn't move to look at who it was. She was safe within her den, and she could scent the person anyway.

Finn.

"Gina?" His voice was right behind her, but she still didn't move.

"Gina? Please. What's wrong?" He knelt in front of her, and she blinked up at him.

"My mate hates me," she whispered. She hadn't meant to whisper, but she couldn't speak louder than that. At the word *mate* coming from her lips, she hiccupped. Mate was a lie. He was only a wolf. A wolf who didn't want her. Who hated her.

An icy feeling spread over her limbs and settled into her heart, which felt like a hollow cavern with no bridge to escape.

"Mate?" Finn asked.

She looked up into his dark green eyes and nodded.

When had he grown up? He wasn't the little boy she'd held in her arms when she'd first joined the family. He was starting to fill out with the muscles of a man, rather than the long lankiness of a grown boy. His dark brown hair went every which way and even touched his shoulders, like his father's hair once had.

"Oh, Gina." With that, he pulled her into his arms and cradled her in his lap. She stuck her nose along his neck and shoulder, inhaling his scent. He was her family, her home. He could make it better.

Oh, goddess, please make it better.

She didn't know how long she stayed in her brother's arms, but she didn't care. She needed to let it all out before she exploded. Other people came to her side. She heard and scented them. Outsiders stayed away, but her family was there. She hated feeling weak, helpless, but if she didn't cry for what she'd lost, what she now knew she'd never have, she'd break more than she already had.

Finn handed her off to someone, and she blinked her eyes open. Kade frowned down at her then stood up.

"We're going home, baby girl, and then you can tell me what happened."

That wasn't the Alpha who'd spoken, but her father still demanded answers. The two parts of him were sometimes hard to tell apart, but right then, she needed her dad. Then she'd need her Alpha.

He carried her three steps, and she pushed at his shoulder. He stopped and looked down at her. She could feel her brothers, mother, cousins, aunts, and uncles around her. The entire Jamenson clan had come to her aid because of her howl, and she'd never felt more loved.

Even when she'd never felt so unwanted.

"I need to walk to our home on my own," she said softly, but stronger than she'd spoken earlier.

She was a dominant wolf. Though she was in pain, she needed to stand on her own two feet in front of the rest of the Pack. If needed, she'd break down again in quiet later.

Kade gave her a nod, his wolf in his eyes, and then set her down. She wobbled for a moment, but with her family behind her, she raised her chin then took a step.

Then another.

Then another.

She moved through the den, ignoring the curious looks from Pack members who either meant well or relished her pain. After all, she was a witch.

A witch who didn't have full control of her powers.

What right did she have to judge them for their wariness of her?

What right did she have to judge Quinn for his reasons not to trust her?

A witch had destroyed his life and was slowly killing his son—she knew his pain was justified.

She just wished it didn't hurt so much.

When she made her way to the front door, she felt the rest of the family slowly leave. Only her brothers and parents remained behind. The other Jamensons seemed to know she needed space from the immense crowd.

She'd never loved them more.

Ben, her youngest brother at ten years old, went around her to open the door. He gave her a small smile then took her hand, pulling her into the house.

Tristan and Drake hurried off to the kitchen while Ben and Nick forced her to sit on the couch. They sat on either side of her, pressing themselves against her so she could feel her family, her Pack. Mark sat on the other side of Ben and leaned in. She wrapped her arms around them and kissed each of their heads. Her brothers were growing up so fast, and soon they'd all be men in their own right.

She loved them so freaking much.

She'd be okay. She had her family, her wolf, and her strength. She'd find a way to prevail and heal. Quinn had lashed out and hurt her more than she thought possible, but she didn't need him. Fate would give her another mate. Maybe not now, maybe not for a decade, but it could happen.

She'd just learn to be herself until then.

She'd done well on her own before, and she'd do it again.

Her mother sat on the coffee table in front of her and put her hands on Gina's knees. "Talk to me, baby."

"We can go if you want to talk with just Mom and Dad," Finn said, surprising her. He had an old soul and could be sweet if he wanted to be, but he was also a very dominant wolf. The fact that he would let her speak about what happened without him there told her how bad she must look. Some things were private, but if Finn wanted to know exactly what had hurt her, he wouldn't have left no matter what. They were walking on eggshells around her, and she wasn't sure she liked that.

She didn't like the fact that Quinn had pushed her into this position.

Damn the wolf.

She shook her head. "No. You can stay." She met her mother's eyes. The pain she saw there made her swallow hard.

Her mom knew.

Maybe not all of it, but she knew.

Tristan and Drake came back into the living room with tea and cookies for everyone. Mel had trained her brood well. Gina took a cookie and a cup of tea, knowing she needed the nutrients. She'd never gotten her meal after shifting and her run with Quinn, and her tired wolf was on edge.

Gina licked her lips and nodded at her mother. "I went to Quinn today to talk about the fact that he's my potential mate."

Kade let out a curse while the boys either hugged her or mumbled one of their own.

Finn gave her a look, frowned, then started to pace.

"You and Quinn," Kade said softly, though his wolf was up front from the sound of his growl.

She nodded. "Yes, me and Quinn." She winced. There wasn't a "her and Quinn," but she'd get to that part.

"I don't want to talk about everything." She met her father's gaze. "I can't. But I will say that he didn't want to be my mate. He had a good reason." A reason that hurt her more than anything, but she'd move on.

Kade growled full-out, and her brothers joined him. Goose bumps rose over her flesh at the sound, so protective yet angry at the same time.

"There isn't a good enough reason to hurt my daughter. You are a Redwood and will one day be the Enforcer. Does he think you're not good enough?"

Yes, but not for the reasons he'd said.

Not that she'd tell him that.

She shook her head instead. "He had a mate, Dad. He had a mate, and now he doesn't. He has a five-year-old son to raise, and finding a new mate isn't on his agenda."

"Oh, honey," Mel whispered then cupped her face. "I'm so sorry."

Gina didn't cry. She didn't think she had anything left to cry about. "It's okay, Mom. I tried. I put myself out there. He didn't want me. I get it. He doesn't want another mate." *He doesn't want a witch*. "There's nothing I can do about it."

"We can beat him up for you," Ben put in.

"Yeah, I'll tie him down," Tristan said.

"No one is allowed to hurt our sister," Drake said.

"We love you, Gina," Mark said. "We don't like it when you cry."

"We really will hurt him for you," Nick added.

She sniffed then kissed each brother, even standing up so she could kiss Finn's cheek. He looked down at her, still frowning.

"I'd kill him if I could," he growled.

She shook her head. "That's the exact wrong thing to do, Finn. You know that."

"I don't care if he's a freaking Talon. He hurt my family. From the way you reacted, it wasn't just a brush-off, Gina. He hurt you."

She closed her eyes. "I know, Finn, but you need to remember that you're the Heir. You can't kill a member of another Pack because he hurt your sister."

"You think I don't get that? You think I don't know that I'm the Heir? I've been the Heir for as long as I can remember, Gina. I'm not going to mess things up for my Pack because of what he did, but that doesn't mean I don't want to. I want to put family first. Can't you get that?"

"We all get that," Kade said from behind her, and she opened her eyes. "You know we all get that. The whole family has had to put some of their own wants and needs on hold because of the war with the Centrals. Now with the treaty with the Talons, we're forced to do that again."

"When Logan and Lexi first joined us, we wanted nothing to do with the Talons," Mel said. "Gina, you might have been old enough to remember when they first came to us. We wanted blood for the way the previous Alpha had treated them, but we had to step back." She cupped Gina's face. "But if we need to, we'll fight for you, Gina. Never forget that you are our daughter. You are Larissa and Neil's daughter. Your heart matters just as much as whatever the Talons mean to us. You matter more. If you want us to take matters into our own hands with this, we will."

"Just because he's a Talon and we're trying to find a way to make our treaty work with them doesn't give him the right to hurt you," Kade said.

She pulled back and shook her head. "I don't want to do anything that will hurt the Talons or the Redwoods. In fact, this is good, right?" She tried to smile and failed. "Okay, so the rejecting thing is horrible, and I'll get over it because I have to, but that's not what I'm talking about. You know we formed the council because of many things, but one of those was because there hadn't been any matings between the Talons and Redwoods in all this time. This is huge."

God, she knew she sounded like an idiot, but if she didn't move on to something she *could* talk about without breaking down, she wouldn't be able to speak at all.

"Gina, you don't have to try to make this better," Mark said from her side.

She shook her head. "I'm not really, but think about it. There's a mating between a Talon and a Redwood. We're moving forward."

"And if the goddess sees you both reject it and doesn't allow another mating?" Finn asked.

Kade growled. "Then that is something we deal with, Finn. We won't force Gina to deal with Quinn for the sake of the Packs."

She blinked. She hadn't thought of that. What if Quinn rejecting her and their potential mating brought them all back a step?

"No, we can't think like that." She took a deep breath. "We need to tell the others about the potential mating. They need to have hope."

Mel shook her head. "Honey, then you'll have to face the world and tell them that you won't be mating him."

She clenched her jaw. "Then Quinn will have to do the same. We are the council leaders. We will show the Packs that we are closer to becoming a strong unit. The others will understand that we chose not to mate. He has a child. He had a mate. That's all they need to know."

They didn't need to know that he'd rejected her for not only that but because she was a witch.

Her palms heated, and she closed them into fists. She was only a half witch. She didn't have full powers. She didn't have the control she needed to use them on a daily basis. Yet he didn't know that. He'd seen only who he thought she was and rejected her in the worst way possible.

For the sake of her Pack, she wouldn't be able to run away from her problems. It wasn't as if she could do that to begin with. Her wolf would never want her to do so.

She was stronger than that. She'd fight for her Pack as well as learn to negotiate and strengthen her Pack.

"Gina, you don't have to do this," Kade said softly.

"Yeah, I do. If I don't, I'll just end up hiding when I don't need to. I know everything hasn't hit me yet, and I'll deal with it when it does, but I need to be strong. I need to be a council and Pack leader. This is good for the den, Dad." She sucked in a breath. "Maybe more matings will come out of it. Maybe more trust."

"Do you really think trust will come out of the fact that Quinn rejected you?" Finn asked, and Gina winced. "Shit. I'm sorry."

"Language, Finn," Mel whispered.

"You didn't stop me before," he said, a small smile on his face.

"We were upset, and I let one pass. Not again."

Gina's mouth twitched. God, she loved her family. They understood her even when she didn't understand herself.

"Finn, he rejected me because he already had a mate." *And he didn't trust me.* "People will understand. It's only been five years. He's not ready."

"Until you find a mate of your own, you'll always feel the mating urge when you are near him," Mel said softly. "Are you going to be able to work with him knowing that?"

She nodded. It was going to be harder than hell, but she was stronger than she gave herself credit for. At least she hoped so.

"We can move you off the council," Kade added.

"Not yet," she said. "I need to work through it all. I mean, I don't understand it yet, and I can't just run away."

Mark hugged her from behind, and in a few moments, her other brothers hugged her as well. Finn stood in front of her, his hands in his pockets and his brow raised.

"You need help, you call," he said. "You know I'll be there in a heartbeat, Heir or no Heir."

She smiled at him then and let another tear fall. "I love you, little brother."

He blushed and ducked his head. "Love you too, big sister." He hugged her, too, as the other boys squeezed her harder. Soon her mom and dad joined in, and her wolf whimpered, rubbing along her skin, needing the contact.

This was her family, her Pack. They would help her heal, so she could move on.

She just hoped that one day she'd be able to face Quinn and not remember his words, not remember the pain.

The wolf had edged his way under her skin, and now she'd have to pry him out.

Once and for all.

Chapter Six

Quinn ran a hand over his head and tried to keep his eyes open. He hadn't slept in forty-eight hours, and his body was starting to feel it. His wolf clawed at his skin, begging to be let out so they could make something bleed, make something feel worse than he did.

His skin itched, and his head pounded. If he didn't keep moving, keep pacing, he was going to either go wolf or pass out. Neither of those would do him any good right then.

"Quinn. Go for a run and let some of that energy out. You're not doing any good here pacing and letting your wolf just get more amped up."

Quinn let out a soft growl at Walker's words. He didn't want the Healer to tell him what to do. The other man might have been more dominant than him, but that didn't mean he was in the right mind-set to deal with it. He didn't want to go on a run and let his wolf burn off their energy.

He wanted his son to be healthy.

He wanted his son to be able to shift.

Claws ripped from his fingertips, and he let out a growl that shook the windows.

"Out!" Walker yelled, his voice sharp, deadly. "Your wolf is taking control, and I won't have you hurting my patient."

Quinn staggered back, his claws receding. His heart pounded, and his jaw dropped. "I would *never* hurt Jesse."

Walker's eyes glowed gold, his wolf coming to the forefront. "I'm sure you think that, but right now? I don't know. I don't know what you'd do by accident. You've been a loose cannon since you kicked Gina out of here, and now with Jesse taking a turn on top of that? I just don't know. Go for a damn run then come back here."

"I'll run with you."

Quinn turned around on his heel at the sound of his Alpha's voice. "You have more important things to do than babysit me, Gideon."

Gideon raised a brow. "First, I'm Alpha. You don't get to tell me what to do. Second, the health and safety of my Pack is the most important thing on my list of worries and duties. So I'm going on a run with you, and we're going to burn off your energy. Then you can come back here and sit with your son."

Quinn let out a whimper, his wolf taking over. He looked at the closed door that hid the bed where his son slept.

"I don't know that I can leave him," he whispered, hating that he voiced his weakness.

Brandon, their Omega, put his hand on Quinn's shoulder, and Quinn immediately relaxed enough to breathe. The other man had the ability to take emotional stress into himself—even if it cost him to do so. Quinn could feel some of the tension sliding out of his shoulders, his heart, and his soul.

"Go," Brandon ordered softly. "We will be here by Jesse's side. If we need you, we'll howl. You'll hear us."

Defeated, Quinn lowered his head then turned toward the front door. He took a deep breath, knowing he was acting like a lunatic. "Thank you for watching my son."

"He's family," Walker said.

With that, he followed Gideon out of the house and toward the clearing where they could shift. On their way, he could hear people milling about around him. Their pitying looks slayed him, but he did his best to ignore them. The others knew Jesse was ill, knew he might not make it through the week, but there was nothing any of them could do.

There was nothing *he* could do.

When they made it to the clearing, it was just him and Gideon, but for all the world, he felt like he was alone. Some of that was his doing, he knew, but not all. He couldn't fix it.

They gave Quinn the space he needed, though it went against their nature to leave a wolf in distress. He couldn't handle too many wolves though. Not right then and maybe not ever. How the hell was he still a lieutenant?

He didn't deserve the title. Didn't deserve the responsibility.

He only wanted his son to be healthy, and yet that seemed to be too much to ask. He'd do anything to give Jesse back his chance at life—only he wasn't sure there was anything he could do, anything he could sacrifice to make that happen.

"We'll figure out what's wrong with him," Gideon said, as if what he ordered would come true.

Quinn couldn't lose hope, but right then, it was hard to see the light at the end of the tunnel when his little boy was sick and in trouble.

"He can't shift, Gideon," he said, his voice breaking. He refused to look weak in front of the other wolves, but this was his Alpha. Gideon already knew everything about him and his strengths.

He still couldn't believe it, couldn't get the image of his son screaming in pain out of his mind. The agony on Jesse's face...

He fell on all fours and threw up, his body shaking.

Gideon ran a hand down Quinn's back as he tried to catch his breath.

"We'll figure it out, Quinn. We're not going to lose him."

Spent, Quinn sat down and rested his forearms on his knees. "I don't know what I'll do if..."

"Stop it. Don't even say it. We're going to figure it out. Now, tell me exactly what happened when it first started."

"I've already told you and Walker. Brandon too." He'd done it without emotion, without looking at them. His eyes had been on Jesse, as if he could will his son to shift and be healthy.

"True, but I want to hear it again. Maybe there's a detail I'm missing. Maybe there is something we can do to slow the progression so we have more time."

Time. God, he just wanted more time. Jesse was only five years old. He deserved more time.

He took a deep breath, his wolf calming down at his Alpha's presence. Maybe he wouldn't need that run after all. Maybe just getting out of the situation for a few minutes would work.

"After Gina left—"

"After you kicked her out," Gideon cut in.

Quinn let out a growl. "You know why I did that."

"Yes. I do. But that doesn't mean you had to do it that way. I haven't heard from Kade yet, but I have a feeling I might."

Quinn closed his eyes and let out a curse. "What happened between me and Gina happened between me and Gina. Not between the Packs. We can't let everything we've tried to do for the strength of our Packs fall apart because we chose not to mate."

Gideon sighed, and Quinn opened his eyes. "True, but you were an asshole according to Walker. There are going to be consequences, but we'll deal with those when the time comes. The fact that you *could* have mated at all is a step in the right direction. You're the first to feel your mate in years, Quinn. Add in the fact it's a cross-Pack potential mating, and it's a good thing."

He swallowed hard and rubbed the spot over his heart. "I can't talk about her, Gideon."

His Alpha leveled him a gaze. "You might not have a choice, but we'll move on for the moment. Tell me what happened after she left."

"Walker reamed me a new one and left."

"Good for him."

"Gideon."

"Keep going."

Quinn sighed. "Like I said, Walker left soon after, and I made dinner for me and Jesse. He hadn't eaten before he'd gone to sleep, so I knew he'd need some protein."

"You'd just shifted with Gina."

"Gideon," he whispered.

"Go on."

"I woke up Jesse, and we ate." Quinn ran a hand over his face. "I could tell he was a little more tired than usual, but I thought it was just because I'd woken him up from his nap. He'd also played with Walker that morning. I thought he was just tired."

"What happened next?"

"We finished eating. Jesse wanted to shift to his wolf because it had been a few days. Normally, that's not a problem, you know, sometimes we just want to let our wolf roam. I didn't want to go to the clearing and deal with people, and if Jesse was still tired, I didn't want to make it worse. So instead, I let Jesse try to shift in the living room." He paused and met Gideon's gaze for a moment before turning away from the power in that stare. "Tried, Gideon. Tried. He couldn't. He screamed like someone was trying to kill him, and I thought I'd died right with him."

Gideon gripped his shoulder. "You got Walker right away and held your son. You did all you could do."

"It wasn't enough." God, *he* wasn't enough.

"It's not your fault, Quinn."

"We're not going there."

"Quinn."

"Fine. It's Helena's fault that Jesse is sick, that he can't shift. I get that. But why did Helena leave, Gideon? Why wasn't I good enough to keep our bond, huh? Did you ever think of that? She left us, took half my soul with her. She hated me enough to risk her own life so she could break our mating bond and then the Pack bonds that held her to the Talons. She left us, Gideon. She left Jesse. So you sit there and tell me that there wasn't anything I could do to keep her. Tell me I didn't do anything to push her away."

He swallowed the bile rising in his throat. He hadn't spoken of his fears in the five years Helena had been gone. He'd been so scared to do so, but those thoughts had been on a loop for all those years.

Something had happened to force Helena to leave him and Jesse. She hadn't just woken up one day and decided to run away from it all.

He must have done something to lose her love, her faith, her trust.

He just didn't know what.

Maybe he'd been too focused on his duties to the Pack. He'd always been a wolf that put other people's needs and wants above his own. He was a dominant wolf, and that meant protecting others no matter the cost. When he was younger and unmated, he'd put his all into finding a way to strengthen the Pack under the former, crueler Alpha.

When Gideon became Alpha, Quinn had risen in the ranks and pledged his life in order to protect what the den would one day become.

He didn't change that ideal when Jesse came along. He and Helena had mated before Gideon became Alpha. She'd stood by his side for twenty years, through thick and thin, through pain, war, and peace.

Then she'd left.

He must have done something.

Just one more reason he would never be with Gina.

He closed his eyes and cursed.

Damn. He wouldn't think about her. He couldn't. He'd pushed her away for her own good. He might have lied to himself and her about the whole witch thing, but in reality, it was only for her. He wasn't a good bet. He wasn't even whole.

If he was honest with himself, he didn't hate her.

He couldn't.

His wolf wouldn't let him.

No, he was *scared* of her.

Scared of not only the powers he didn't understand, but scared of what she could become to him.

He closed his eyes, aware his Alpha was staring at him as he got lost in his own head. If he allowed himself to get close to Gina, allowed himself to bond again, what was to say she wouldn't just leave him like

Helena had? He'd already been through that once. He wasn't sure he was strong enough to go through that again.

Plus, with Gina...there was something about her that called to him on a different level than Helena had, and that scared him more than he wanted to admit.

He'd hurt her to make sure she could never hurt him.

He was an asshole and he knew that in order for them to be able to work together again, he'd have to apologize. He just wasn't sure he deserved her forgiveness.

No, he *knew* he didn't deserve anything along those lines.

He'd fucked up with Gina for their own good. That didn't mean it had to *feel* good.

He sighed then opened his eyes. "I'm ready to go back," he said softly.

Gideon studied his face. "I think you are, but first, I need to tell you what will happen next."

Quinn frowned and tilted his head. "What do you mean? What's going on?"

His Alpha let out a breath. "Walker isn't sure what will happen next, and he's asked for help. I gave him my blessing, Quinn."

Quinn stood up on shaky legs. "He called Hannah, didn't he?"

Gideon stood slowly so they were almost eye-to-eye. "Yes, he had to. Hannah is a Healer as well. She might be able to see something Walker can't. Or maybe the two of them together can work on a different level than they can alone. The fact that she's also a witch adds another layer to her powers."

Witch.

Something must have shown on his face because Gideon cursed then threw a punch.

The right side of Quinn's face burned, and he blinked but refused to touch the place where Gideon's fist had connected.

"You're kidding me, right?" Gideon yelled. "*That's* why you threw Gina away? That? I always knew you had some issues with powers outside of being a wolf, but I never knew you were a bigot. She's a half witch, you asshole. Half. She's learning her powers at Hannah's side. And even if she was a full witch, she could have been your *mate*. That trumps any preconceived notions you have about something you don't truly understand. I've never been more disappointed in you. Never."

Quinn lowered his head, his shoulders dropping. His wolf howled, but he didn't make a sound. He'd disappointed his Alpha, himself, and anyone who had relied on him.

He *knew* that, yet he'd thrown away his chance because he was goddamn scared.

Scared of what could happen, scared of the unknown, scared of a blue-eyed wolf who haunted him.

"I'm sorry, my Alpha."

Gideon gripped the back of his neck, and Quinn lowered himself further. "You don't need to be sorry to me, Quinn. You need to apologize to Gina and actually mean it. You need to get over what Helena did to you. Yeah, I'm a prick for saying it, but it needs to be said. She hurt you. She hurt Jesse. She hurt all of us. But if you don't learn to break through that pain and find some peace on the other side, you're no good to us."

"I don't know if I can," he said honestly.

"Look at me, Quinn."

Quinn raised his head and looked at his Alpha's face, though he didn't meet his eyes. There were only so many dominance games a wolf could play, and this was not one of them. Not today.

"You messed up. You need to fix it. Also, if you *ever* treat a witch the way you did Gina, there will be consequences you can't get out of. You understand me?"

Quinn sucked in a breath but nodded. "I do. I screwed up. Bad. I just..." He shook his head. "No excuses. There was more than one reason I said no to Gina, but I used the one I shouldn't have to be cruel. For that I will apologize the next time I see her."

Gideon searched his face. "Good, because you're about to see her real soon."

Quinn took a step back. "What?"

"She's coming with Hannah as her aide. In fact, they might already be there. You calm enough to see her? Or do you need that run?"

Quinn blinked then ran a hand over his head. "I'm good. I think I just needed to get out of the house." And to be near his Alpha, but that was understood.

"Good. Don't screw up again. I'll be with you. We're not leaving you alone with Gina right now. I hope you get that."

Quinn nodded. It hurt for some reason, yet he knew it was deserved. "I just want Jesse to be healthy. I'll do anything, Gideon."

Gideon's face fell. "I know. Come on. Let's see what we can do to save your little boy."

They ran back to Quinn's place, each in their own head. He didn't know what Gideon was thinking about, but Quinn's thoughts were running the gamut. Between Jesse, Gideon's disappointment, and Gina, his mind whirled. He hadn't slept in two days, but he was energized on the idea that there would be people here to try to help his son.

That was worth any pain he might have from seeing the woman his wolf wanted but couldn't have.

The fact that he couldn't have her because he'd pushed her away was his own damn fault.

When they walked into his house, he scented her. That sweetness filled his nostrils and sent his wolf on edge. He pushed it away though. He didn't deserve any bliss that came from her presence. Instead, he deserved the torture and pain that it brought.

Three other scents mingled together alongside Gina's wolf, and his wolf perked. They were not Talons. No, those were Redwoods. Gideon hadn't mentioned more than Gina and Hannah, but he shouldn't have been surprised at who had come with them. Where Hannah went, her two mates, Reed and Josh, followed. She might have been allowed to leave with just one of them on her own, but coming to a different Pack den wouldn't have allowed either man to stay behind.

He understood that devotion and love, even envied it.

He pushed all of that away though when he stepped into his master bedroom. Jesse had apparently been moved there when he'd been out, but it made sense. There were far too many wolves to fit into Jesse's room now.

"Thank you for coming," Quinn said when he walked into the room. He was surprised his voice didn't shake or turn into a growl, but he knew he needed to keep up his control.

Each person turned toward him, their gazes burning holes into his skin. Jesse lay on the bed, propped up on pillows. He was awake, thank God, so Quinn smiled but didn't move forward. He needed to get a few things out of the way first.

Walker and Brandon stood off to the right. Walker had his hands out in front of him, stretching, while Brandon had his arms folded over his chest. They didn't frown at him, but they did seem to check him out to make sure he wasn't about to go on attack.

He'd deal with that shame later.

To the left, Hannah had her hands in a similar position to Walker's. Her long brown curls went every which way and looked like she'd been in the wind.

Reed stood behind Hannah, his hands on her hips. Quinn knew that the touch of a mate could enhance their powers, so he was glad the other man was there. Josh stood beside Reed. He didn't touch Hannah but looked ready to do so if needed. The triad as a whole, it was said, was the strongest unit most had ever heard of when it came to magic. In fact, each of the Jamenson mating pairs—or triads—seemed to gain a certain amount of power from their bond.

Something he'd never had with Helena.

He quickly shoved that thought to the side and looked at the person on the other side of Josh.

Gina had her hair back in a ponytail, which made her look younger than her years. Her cheekbones stood out, and from the dark circles under her eyes, she looked as though she'd slept as well as he had these past two days.

Your fault, he reminded himself.

From the way she held herself back, he wasn't sure she had the energy to help Jesse. God knew Quinn didn't have much left himself. He didn't want Gina to be hurt because she pushed herself too hard, but he wasn't about to say that aloud.

He didn't have the right.

He cleared his throat. "I don't know what I should be doing." He looked at Walker then at Hannah, pulling his gaze from Gina's. "Can you tell me where I should stand? What I should do?"

He hated being helpless, but he'd do anything for Jesse.

"Daddy," Jesse whispered, and Quinn broke. He quickly knelt on the bed and reached over to grip Jesse's hand.

"Hey, buddy."

"I'm sorry," he said softly.

Tears burned, and Quinn blinked them away. He would not cry in front of his son. "For what? You did nothing wrong. Hannah and her crew are just here to see if there's anything they can do. I'm going to be here for you, Jesse. No matter what."

That he vowed.

"Jesse, honey, you're doing good," Hannah said, her voice melodic. "Walker and I are going to try to use that same Healing power he used on you before, but together this time."

Jesse turned his head toward her slowly, as if it hurt to move.

Quinn's wolf howled.

"It feels warm when he does that. Will it hurt this time?"

"No, honey, it won't."

From the way Hannah said that, Quinn knew there was something else going on. He knew from talking with Walker that there should have been pain each time Walker tried to Heal Jesse, but he brought that pain into himself. Hannah, it seemed, would be doing the same. From the looks on Reed's and Josh's faces, the two men would be syphoning what they could off as well so Hannah wouldn't be hurt.

"I am grateful," Quinn said, looking at the triad, then his Talons, then Gina. "Thank you for coming here and helping." Thank you for taking the pain he could not.

"We wouldn't be anywhere else," Gina said softly, and Quinn forced himself not to move toward her and beg for forgiveness.

"Jesse, honey, I'm going to let your mind sleep for a bit so we can work," Hannah said after a moment. "You won't feel a thing, and before you know it, you'll be awake."

His son looked frightened for a moment then nodded. "Daddy? You'll be here when I wake up?"

"Always."

Hannah and Walker held out their arms over Jesse, and his little boy's eyes lowered.

The Redwood Pack Healer let out a breath. "Now that he's asleep, I'm going to explain what's going to happen. Okay?"

Quinn nodded. "Anything. Just tell me what I need to do."

Hannah looked pained for a moment then nodded. "We're going to try to Heal him, or at least keep the pain from growing worse. The fact that this is happening at a fundamental level due to the bond break means there might not be anything else to do."

Quinn growled then backed off at the look in Reed's and Josh's eyes. "I'm sorry. I didn't want to hear that."

Hannah gave him a sad smile. "I don't want to hear that. What I *do* think we can do is create a web of energy to try and fortify what he has. Meaning we can take away his pain and let him lead a normal life. It won't be permanent, but it might give him enough time to find a mate of his own when he grows older."

Hope filled him. "That could Heal him?"

Hannah shook her head. "I don't know. That's one way. Another way is if you mate again."

He felt as if he'd been shot. He could feel Gina by his side but refused to look at her.

"You're saying if I mate again, I could save my son?"

Hannah held up her hand. "I'm saying that it could happen. Your son is sick because Helena performed the worst kind of betrayal imaginable. Walker and I have been talking, and we think that if you create a new bond, there's a slight possibility it could attach itself to Jesse."

Quinn turned to Walker. "You knew? And you didn't say anything?" Still, he didn't look at Gina.

"We weren't sure," Walker said softly.

"Quinn. We can deal with that later," Hannah cut in. "First, let me explain what is going to happen now."

He nodded, forcing his gaze to Hannah while his mind whirled. If he mated with another wolf, he could save his son. He knew he wasn't ready for a bond, but to save Jesse? He'd do anything.

Yet he didn't deserve Gina's bond.

He'd fucked himself over so well he didn't see a way out of it.

"We're going to take his pain and Heal him as best we can for now," Hannah continued. "But to create the web, Brandon and Gideon will act as conduits for Walker while Reed and Josh do the same for me. We can enhance our magic that way." She met Quinn's eyes full on. "You'll need to hold Jesse's hand and create a point of magic yourself. However, you can't do it alone. You'll need a witch to aid you."

He swallowed hard then finally looked at Gina. Her eyes were wide, and she looked shell-shocked.

"Tell me what to do, Aunt Hannah," she said, her voice strong.

He could love her if he'd let himself, if he was willing to go down that path. He honestly couldn't think of that though. He couldn't think of himself. This was all for Jesse. He needed to remember that.

Hannah gave her niece a nod. "Sit on the bed next to Quinn and hold his hand. Gideon will put his hand on Quinn's shoulder while Josh will do the same to yours. We'll create our circle, our web, and then we will try for the best."

With that, everyone got into position. Gina's leg rested against his, and he did his best not to groan.

"Gina…"

She shook her head. "No. Not now. Later. We can talk about everything later. Right now, this is for Jesse. It's all about Jesse."

He nodded, swallowing hard. He didn't deserve a woman like her, and they all knew it. He also didn't know what the future held, but he'd do whatever he could to protect his son.

He held out his hand, and Gina paused for only a moment before placing hers in his. The heat shocked him, and he sucked in a breath, his wolf raging at him.

"For Jesse," she whispered.

For Jesse.

Chapter Seven

"Begin."

At the sound of Hannah's voice, Gina threw her head back. Power slammed into her, and she gripped Quinn's hand. She hated herself for craving his touch, craving his need. Then she pushed that away, knowing this wasn't about her and Quinn, but about a little boy who needed them both.

Magic filled her body, scraping along her skin before wrapping around her organs. The hair on her arms rose, and she tried to swallow, only to come up dry. She'd never felt this much power before. It wasn't as if she was a strong witch. No, she was a strong *wolf* who happened to spew fire from her palms when she thought real hard about it. There was a difference.

She forced herself to look down at Quinn's son and what was happening in front of her. Hannah and Walker chanted over Jesse, their arms moving in unison as they pulled on their bonds to Heal him. Josh and Reed had their arms around Hannah's waist, holding her steady. Brandon and Gideon had their hands on their brother's shoulders, keeping him still. Quinn sucked in a breath next to her, and she braced herself. A wave of pain crashed into her, and she bit her lip. The fire in her veins blended with her magic and wove a spell around the pain, dissipating it.

She didn't know how she did that, only that it was inherent. Her birth mother had taught her enough to protect herself and other people, but they hadn't gotten to the lessons about *using* her powers.

She wasn't a Healer, nor was she a witch who could help others. At least that's what she thought. It wasn't as if she'd seen any evidence to the contrary. She could only use what she knew, and that was to take whatever pain Jesse, and subsequently Quinn, held and make it go away.

She kept her eyes open and on Jesse. If she focused on him, she could deal with the pain and anything that came afterward. She licked her lips, knowing if she broke her concentration she'd ruin it for all of them. She couldn't—wouldn't—be that weak link.

The process took hours, and by the end of it, she was drained, emotionally and physically. Sweat covered her body, and she had a hard time staying upright. She blinked a couple of times, then sucked in a breath when Quinn leaned into her, thereby keeping her from passing out. She looked down and swallowed hard.

Throughout it all, though, she never let go of Quinn's hand.

Hannah's earlier words echoed through her head, but she ignored them, pushing them away. There would be time to make decisions and deal with the consequences of a woman's betrayal. A woman Gina had never met.

Gina's pain and loss would be worth the life of a young boy.

She knew that, but she didn't want to think of it.

Not yet.

"That's all we can do," Hannah said softly, her voice tired.

Gina leaned into Quinn, her hand still in his. She didn't want to think too hard about it, the feel and scent of him against her. She needed only his strength so she didn't pass out.

"How is he?" Quinn growled out. His wolf sounded close to the surface, but Gina had a feeling it was only because of the exhaustion weighing on all of them.

Walker sighed. "The bond between him and me as a Healer seemed slightly stronger, Quinn. That's a good thing. He isn't in pain right now." He met Quinn's eyes, and Gina squeezed Quinn's hand. She might not know what she felt right then, but she knew the father, not the man who hated her, needed support.

"I think, between this group, we gave him more time," Hannah said slowly.

More time.

That was something at least. Time for what though? That was the question. Either it was enough time for him to find his own mate or for Quinn to try to mate on his own and provide another bond for Jesse to latch onto.

Every single person in the room knew what the answer had to be.

Every single person knew who would supply that answer.

Anything else would be horrific for that little boy.

She'd just have to deal with the consequences.

She let out a breath then released Quinn's hand. Her wolf whimpered, but she ignored it. This was not the time to deal with anything but sleep and her own thoughts. The loss of the heat of Quinn's touch was something she'd have to push away for the time being.

Maybe forever.

"Thank you," Quinn said, this time his voice sounding more himself. "Thank you for doing all you can."

"He's a pup. He's one of us," Hannah said simply.

The others gave her a look then quietly left after saying good-bye and giving Quinn instructions about when Jesse would wake up.

Uncle Josh leaned down, kissed her temple, whispering so low that only she could hear. "We're not leaving you. We'll be right outside."

With that, she, Jesse, and Quinn were alone in the room. She got up off the bed, her legs shaky. She hadn't been sleeping or eating right in the past couple of days, and with the added-on magic, her body was feeling it. She knew she needed to take better care of herself, but it had been hard when her heart hadn't been in it.

Now she didn't have a choice.

"I'm going to go home and eat and rest," she said finally. Quinn had his eyes on his son, not her, so it made it easer for her to speak.

He turned toward her, and her mouth went dry.

His wolf was in his gaze, the gold rim around his irises glowing. "Thank you," he said, his voice strong. "Thank you for coming here when you didn't have to and saving my son. I will never be able to repay you for that."

She raised her chin, her heart pounding even as her soul died just that much more. "I wasn't going to let a pup be hurt because of my—no, your—issues." There. She felt a smidge better. Not much, but at least she wasn't lying to herself.

Quinn's jaw tightened, and he nodded. "Thank you anyway." He let out a breath and looked down at his son. "Gina..."

He was going to ask her. After all he'd done to her, after all he'd said, he was going to ask her about the mating. She *knew* they would have to in order to save Jesse's life, but she didn't know if she could handle hearing it in her weakened state.

She raised her hand and stopped him. "I'm going home to sleep and to eat. We can talk about everything that was said here and previously after we're rested." She paused and looked at Jesse. "He's more important than anything, Quinn. I get that. But right now? I'm not in the right state of mind to talk about anything. I hope you get that."

Hope and something else she couldn't quite place flittered through his gaze before he nodded and stood.

"I'll come to you this time," he said softly. "Tomorrow?"

She shook her head. "We'll meet in neutral territory." She shrugged at his look. "My family isn't in your fan club right now, and I don't want to test them."

He nodded. "I understand." He let out a breath. "Tomorrow okay though?"

"Yes. In neutral territory after sunrise, so we can get it over with."

Not the best way to talk about mating someone who was supposed to be her soul mate, but at this point, she couldn't put too much emotion into it. If she did, she'd lose whatever part of herself she had left.

"We can talk about what we need to talk about," she said, being vague. "Council matters can come later."

He let out a breath. "It's getting complicated."

She gave him a sad smile. "It was always complicated, Quinn. Don't lie to yourself."

With one last look at a sleeping Jesse, she left the room and then the house. She passed the Talons, not looking at them. She didn't want to see the questions in their eyes, or the pity.

Her family waited for her on the front porch, and she moved out of the way of their touch. If she let them hug her, console her, she'd break. She only had to make it to the car outside the wards, and then she could cry until she made it into the Redwood wards.

She could do that.

She was far stronger than she felt.

At least she hoped so.

By the next morning, she was slightly more energized and ready to get this talk over with. While she might have stayed up all night thinking, Hannah and her mother hadn't let that happen. Instead, her family fed her then made her drink tea that would make her sleep deeply. Thank the goddess she did because she wasn't sure she'd have made it here this morning if she'd stayed up all night tossing and turning.

What she was about to agree to was going to kill a small part of her. She *knew* that, but she didn't see another choice. She ran a hand over her hair, trying to center herself.

When she was a young girl, she'd been afraid of mating, though she'd never said it out loud. She'd been afraid of finding a wolf, falling in love, and creating a bond. Because once she did that, she'd have children, and those children could be left alone if she died.

Her birth parents died because a traitor had used them to try to frame another wolf for their deaths. The traitor had died painfully, as had the wolves that had used him in the first place, but in some ways, it would never be enough.

She'd never be held by her mother, never be lifted off the ground by her father again. She'd had more years with the both of them than Mark ever had, but those years hadn't been enough.

Melanie and Kade had brought her into their home without a second thought. They'd helped nurture her wolf and her soul while trying to find a way to balance the magic within her veins. They'd never judged her for what she could do if she lost control.

She was a fire witch. A deadly one if she ever tried to use her powers for dark, rather than light. She could use the flame to burn those in her path or, if she focused hard enough, control a flame already made.

She'd used that inner flame to help Heal Jesse, and yet that magic hadn't been enough to save him fully.

No, that would only come from a bond. At least that's what people thought. Hannah and Walker had spent months working on a plan behind Quinn's back so they wouldn't get his hopes up, and now the plan seemed to be a potential mate.

Her.

She swallowed hard.

Even three days ago, she'd have leapt headfirst into the mating without a second thought. Fate and the moon goddess would provide for her, and she would come out ahead, with a mate and child that she could cherish...and would cherish her.

Now she wouldn't have that.

She'd put her heart on the line to talk with Quinn about what *could* happen before she'd known the full extent of Jesse's illness, and she'd come back shattered. Quinn didn't want her. He wanted nothing to do with another woman since the one he'd loved had almost killed him in every way possible. He especially wanted nothing to do with a witch considering *how* Helena had been able to leave him and Jesse.

The fact that Quinn had been desperate enough to save his son that he'd allowed not only Hannah, but Gina as well, into his home to perform magic was not lost on her.

Quinn would do anything for his son.

Including mate the one person he refused to want.

Her.

She sucked in a breath and looked down at her hands. Mating was supposed to be full of love, hope, and promise. Not dread and loss. She was going to mate with Quinn because it was the right thing to do, the only thing to do, and yet it would kill her.

Her wolf nudged at her, and she closed her eyes. Her wolf desperately wanted Quinn and his wolf, and now her wolf would be happy.

At least as happy as she could be within Gina.

Gina would sacrifice her happiness and be in a loveless mating to save Quinn's son.

She couldn't *not* do it.

But she wasn't sure she knew who she'd become at the other end of it.

The scent of six unfamiliar wolves filled her nostrils, and her wolf went on alert. She opened her eyes and felt around with her senses to figure out where the scents were coming from. When she inhaled again, she relaxed, but only marginally.

Three were Redwoods while the other three were Talons—however, her wolf didn't trust them. There was something about the way they came upon her alone on neutral territory that set her on edge.

When the six came out from the cover of trees, she raised her chin. She didn't recognize three of the males. The other three looked familiar, but she didn't know them well. They were all older than her, but lower in rank. Though they lived in an age where women were treated as equals in some respects, wolves, older wolves in particular, had a problem with strong female leaders.

She'd been in more than one dominance fight to prove her worth, and from the tension in the air, she might just have to do that again. The fact that the Talons and Redwoods were working together might have made her happy later, considering she was a leader on the council, but right then, she needed to focus on what was happening in front of her.

"What can I do for you?" she asked, her voice calm. She didn't let her wolf rise to the surface, but she was there, just in case.

The largest Talon wolf stepped forward, and she bristled. "I heard you used your powers to save the little boy."

She didn't frown, but it was close. This was about her powers? Well, shit.

"Yes. You heard correctly." She wouldn't lie to them, but she had a feeling she needed to be careful.

"We always knew you were a witch and a wolf, but you never showed your powers," one of the Redwoods said.

"I don't know if I like the fact that you don't know what you're doing with your fire power, and yet you're touching our children," one of the other Talons put in.

She growled. "I don't know if I care what you like, wolf."

The six came closer, forming a horseshoe around her. Silly wolves. She could take all six of them down, and they knew it. However, if they worked together, it would prove a challenge.

"You're not in control of your powers, and you think you're better than us because you got lucky enough to get adopted," a Redwood said.

She growled again, her wolf rising to the surface. "My birth parents died protecting our Pack. I wouldn't count that as lucky. Now if you're here to fight me because you're a jealous little pup, fine. I'll fight you and win, but this isn't a dominance challenge. I'm stronger than all of you, and you know it. If you didn't, you wouldn't be here as a group. You'll deal with the consequences of fighting outside a match if you provoke me."

The first Talon snorted. "Running back to Mommy and Daddy Alpha? Some wolf you are."

She snarled. "Fuck off, Talons. I thought we were trying to support trust. You call coming up on a lone wolf in neutral territory trust?"

The Talon wolf shrugged. "We trust some of you, but we don't trust you. Witch. Your kind hurt Quinn and the entire Central Pack. We don't like you."

Freaking bigots.

"What's going on here?" Quinn said as he came up from behind her.

He'd been downwind, so she hadn't scented him. However, because her wolf wanted him so, she didn't jump.

Thank the goddess.

"This is the wolf that used her powers," the quietest Talon wolf said. "We want to make sure she doesn't use them again. She doesn't know what she's doing."

Gina let her wolf rise fully, and she growled, sending out her power. The three Redwoods opened their eyes, shocked, and then went to their knees.

They were not humans. They were wolves. One did *not* mess with a more dominant wolf. Witch or not.

She dismissed the Redwoods then turned to the Talons. She held open her palms and let a small spark arc through her. It lasted for only a moment, but it gave enough of a show to bring fear into the other wolves' eyes.

Quinn growled and sent his wolf out. The Talons knelt, and she smiled. It wasn't a nice smile.

"I'm a witch. Get over it. All of you." She was talking to Quinn as well, but she refused to look at him. "I'm your dominant. I'm higher ranking. You don't get to throw a fit because you don't understand something. Ready to go on the attack here because you don't like the family that took me in? Shame on all of you." She turned to the Redwoods. "We'll deal with you in the den. Now get the hell out of my face."

They scurried away, and she knew she'd have to keep an eye on them.

"Same with you three. Go to Mitchell." The three other wolves whimpered then ran toward their den.

When they were alone, Gina sighed and relaxed then stiffened again once she remembered *why* she and Quinn were meeting.

"What was that about?" Quinn asked.

Gina turned to him and raised a brow. "That was about bigotry and ignorance. We have witches in our den, but not many since there aren't many witches out there in the first place. Not everyone trusts them because of what happened with the Centrals all those years ago. It's getting better, but it takes time. As for me personally? They don't like me because they think I got my power through *luck*."

Quinn snarled. "Luck? Your parents fucking died. That's not luck. That's a twist of fate that kicks you in the nuts."

She snorted despite herself. "Eloquent." She sobered then met his gaze. "I meant what I said about my blood. I'm a witch, Quinn. That's never going to change."

He nodded, his face solemn. "I know. For what it's worth, Gina, I'm sorry for saying what I did."

The words were nice, but his original words couldn't be erased. "But not what you felt."

He ran a hand over his head. "I don't know what I feel. And before you think I'm here only because of what Walker said, you're wrong. I felt like an asshole as soon as I said the words. No matter what happened to me before, that doesn't make it your fault. I *do* have issues with witches. But in reality, I have issues with one witch. And with Helena, for that matter. I shouldn't put my own faults and past issues on your shoulders.

That was wrong of me."

She didn't say anything; she wasn't sure she could. While what he said should have made her feel better, she couldn't allow herself to forget. To forgive. For all she knew, he was only saying this because he wanted her to save his son.

That was the problem with being broken by the one person who was supposed to treasure you above all else. She couldn't trust his intentions. Couldn't trust any feelings he might have for her now or one day in the future. Ironic since they'd been brought together to find trust and understanding in the first place.

Yet she would mate with him anyway.

Apparently, she was a glutton for punishment.

"I'm glad you said that, but I don't know if I believe it." She might not trust him, but she would be honest, no matter what. It was the one way she could live through this.

He flinched but nodded. "I understand. I don't deserve anything you could do for me, Gina."

She closed her eyes and took a deep breath. "Jesse needs you to mate again so he can have a fighting chance. I get that."

"Gina..." He paused then sighed. "I can't ask you to do this. I can't ask you to risk your future because of something that you had nothing to do with in the first place."

Rejection stung again, but she pushed it away. Still, his wolf didn't want her. Even though Jesse could live if she risked her happiness to mate with Quinn, the wolf didn't want her.

Well, too damn bad.

"Don't be an idiot. Your son deserves to live. Plus, if we mate, we'll keep the Talons and Redwoods together in another way." She paused. "Though this means that one of us will have to switch Packs. You get that, right? We can't have a mating bond and different Pack bonds. I don't think we have to do it right away, while we're letting the bond settle, but it would have to happen sooner or later." Hell, this was getting more and more complicated. The idea she'd have to leave her family made her want to throw up, but she held herself in check.

Quinn blinked. "I didn't think about that. Well, okay then. Jesse and I will become Redwoods, if they let us in. You're going to be the Enforcer, Gina. There's no way we'd take that from you. Once Jesse gets stronger, we can break the Talon bonds and make our vows to Kade and the Redwoods." He sucked in a breath. "Shit. I can't believe we're talking about this. Gina...I don't want you to give up a future with a man you could love for me."

She shook her head, even as her heart was breaking. "I'm not giving up anything for you, Quinn. I'm doing it all for Jesse. You get that? You're nothing to me. You can't be more. You said I was the epitome of everything you hate, and even if you didn't mean that, you still said it. You can't take those words back. So, yes, I will create a mating bond with you. I will let your wolf mark me as I mark you. I will let you into my body and into my life. I will even let our souls entwine so Jesse can live." She paused. "I will never love you. I can't love a man who hates who and what I am. You don't want my love anyway. You don't want another mate. We will both survive for your son. It's all we can do."

Even as she said the words, she knew she was lying. She'd be honest about everything but that. She had to save part of herself or she'd never make it. She could love this man. He was strong, loyal, and everything she'd ever dreamed of in a mate. Yet she knew she couldn't allow herself to fall. Once she fell, she'd lose everything else she had within her.

Quinn let out a breath. "You're willing to give up everything for my son, Gina. I...I don't know how to repay that."

She raised her chin. "Be a better man and wolf. Raise your son to be a great man. That's all you can do." She closed her eyes and rubbed her temple. "I want to get this over with before I change my mind."

Not the most romantic way to get a wolf into bed, but she was past romance, past caring. She hurt too much to even try.

Quinn let out a breath. "Jesse is at Walker's and will be for the night. They wanted to keep an eye on him. We can go back to my place and..."

"Yeah...and..." She snorted. "We're going to be mates, Quinn. We should at least say what we're going to do."

Quinn met her gaze. "We're going to go back to my place, and I'm going to mark you then fill you with my cock and create a mating bond. You might not love me, Gina, but I'll do everything in my power to show you that I'm worth this. That I'm worthy of you." He took a breath then swallowed hard. She watched his throat work, scared of what he'd say next. "I want you to be happy, Gina."

That's what she was afraid of.

She didn't react. She couldn't. Her wolf howled, and her body ached for the man in front of her.

Her heart, however, fractured that much more.

Chapter Eight

Quinn stared at his hands, not knowing what else to do. It wasn't as if he was a young pup who'd never been in the presence of a woman, but this was different.

This was unheard of.

What the hell was he supposed to do now?

They were in his home, his kitchen, yet he felt like they were on another planet. One where nothing made sense, and yet it had to somehow.

"This is awkward."

Quinn snorted and looked up at Gina. "Yeah. I guess it is."

She ran a hand through her hair, the long brown strands touching the top of her breasts. Honest to God, she looked scared, not ready to entwine her life and soul with him.

"I...I don't know what to do. I've never done this before."

Quinn had been in the process of turning toward the fridge, but ran into the kitchen island at her words. He cursed then blinked up at her.

"Never?"

She narrowed her eyes then rolled them. "I meant I've been with someone before. I'm not a virgin, if that's what you're wondering."

For some reason, his wolf growled at her words. Well, he *knew* the reason. The idea of her with another male made him want to rip the bastard limb from limb, a response that didn't sit lightly with him considering he'd been mated before. Hell, he had a kid. He was a couple of decades older than Gina, so it wasn't like either of them was pure and innocent.

He hadn't really thought of her past.

He hadn't thought of her future either.

Yet here he was, ready to take her future away to save his son. Gina was a far better wolf than he was. He didn't deserve her, and both of them were aware it, yet he knew he couldn't reject her offer.

Not when it could save Jesse.

"Sorry," he mumbled and turned toward the fridge, this time avoiding the island. "Want something to eat?" Maybe if they actually did something other than stare at each other, they could figure out what to do next.

Gina let out a breath. "Yeah. I was too nervous to think about food before I left, and now I'm regretting it."

He just prayed she didn't regret anything else. He pushed that thought out of his head and pulled out vegetables and a steak he had thawing in the fridge.

"I can make us up a steak omelet if you want," he said, trying to sound casual but failing.

"I'll help."

They were so polite and distant. They didn't sound like two wolves who were going to end up in his bedroom, sweaty and soul-bound. The thing was, they didn't know each other. They knew only some of the specifics, but not any of the details that made the human part of their souls want to mate. Their wolves might be ready, and the outcome of Jesse living put a spin on it that changed things, but their human halves were far from ready to be mated for the rest of their eternities.

For one thing, he'd promised himself—and Gina for that matter—that he'd never mate again. He all but threw her out of his house and hurt her more than he'd meant to. Or, rather, he'd hurt her *exactly* like he'd meant to, even if he hadn't wanted to when he truly thought about it.

Quinn pushed those thoughts away and went to the island. "You want to wash the vegetables while I start on the meat?"

"That I can do," she said softly. He noticed the shaking in her hands, but he didn't comment on it. They needed to move past the tension and figure out how the hell they were going to make this work.

He started cutting the meat while heating up oil in the pan. Once he finished that, he got started on the eggs, trying not to notice how good Gina felt next to him. They worked side by side in silence for a few minutes when she came back to the island.

He let out a breath, knowing if he didn't say something, they'd never move past this. "I'm not going to ask if you're sure, Gina," he said softly.

"If I keep asking that, you're either going to punch me or just walk away, and I don't want either of those." He met her gaze, and she widened her eyes.

No, he didn't want her gone, but he wasn't sure of his own motives. Yes, he wanted his son to have a fighting chance, but right then, Jesse wasn't in the room. This was about Quinn and Gina.

And that scared the hell out of him.

"I'm sure, Quinn. I'm not going to back down because it's hard." Her voice didn't hold a hint of anything but strength. For that he could have kissed her.

And he *would*.

Jesus, how the hell had he gotten himself into this situation?

Fate fucking hated him.

"What do you want out of this?" he asked then shook his head at the anger in her eyes. "I don't mean anything bad by it. I mean, what do you want to do with what's happening? We're going to eat breakfast and try to calm ourselves, but at some point, we're going to go back to my bedroom and have sex. You get that, right? This isn't how most matings go, and I feel like I'm taking something important away from you."

She sighed. "Stop it, Quinn. Didn't you just say you wouldn't ask if I was sure? Because what you said sounds a lot like it. As for what I want? I want your son to be happy and healthy. I want my Pack to be safe. I want the Talons to be safe."

He set the beef in the pan, ignoring the sizzle of oil as it popped at him. "You didn't mention what you wanted for yourself."

"No, I guess I didn't. What I wanted before I met you doesn't really matter anymore. What I want now is to find a way to be happy. You don't love me, and I don't love you. We're wolves, not humans. We can find a way to enjoy sex and not hate ourselves for it. As for what comes after a few years of us being together?" She shrugged. "I don't know, but I know I'm not going to punish you for it. You're punishing yourself enough for it."

Goddess, this woman was something else. She was so strong, yet he didn't think she knew it. He turned the heat down on the stove then moved to wash his hands. After he dried them, he prowled toward her. She stood as stiff as a statue, yet he didn't stop. When he cupped her cheek, she parted her lips.

"You are something else, Gina. You are the strongest wolf I know, and I've met a lot of strong wolves. The fact you're sacrificing a future you could have for Jesse..." He let out a breath. "I don't think I could ever repay you."

She licked her lips, and his gaze followed the movement. "Just don't hate me," she said so low he wasn't sure he heard her right.

His thumb rubbed her cheek, and he nodded slowly. "I don't hate you, Gina." She sucked in a breath, and he cursed himself for his rage before. "I hate what Helena and the witch who helped her did to me. Did to Jesse. But I don't hate you."

She met his gaze, and he hoped she saw the truth in his words. "Don't hate who I am, then. Can you do that? Can you get over what happened and know that I'm wolf, witch, and woman?"

He searched her face for a long while then nodded, knowing it was the truth. "I can do that, Gina. I can treat you as Gina, if you can treat me as Quinn. Can you forgive me?"

She lifted up on her toes then brushed her lips against his. His wolf pressed against his skin, craving more. "You need to stir the meat," she said once she went back to the flat of her feet. "I'll start the eggs."

He hesitated, then nodded. She hadn't said she'd forgiven him, but he didn't blame her. He'd cut right to the bone, but he'd do everything in his power to prove that he was worthy of her…even if he couldn't risk his heart.

He'd already lost everything, and he didn't know if he could do it again. Not fully. Only time would tell.

They finished making breakfast while speaking of Pack duties and council matters. They didn't discuss what would happen next or even what would happen the next day. Things were going to change in every way possible. He was going to leave his Pack, his home, and his friends to protect his son. The fact that he would so willingly do that shocked him, yet he knew it shouldn't have.

Jesse was more important than anything.

Even himself.

After breakfast, they did the dishes and then stood next to one another, the tension rising again. He cupped her face and let out a breath when she let him, this time even leaning into his palm.

"You know the two steps of mating, right?" he asked, his voice low. Best to get the formalities out of the way since they were both nervous.

She nodded. "We will each mark one another so our wolves will be bonded, and then when we make love, you'll release inside me, sealing the other half of the bond."

Make love.

He liked those words on her lips.

It sounded better than fucking or sex. It sounded as if they were actually going to try and be normal rather than going about this in all the worst ways possible.

He nodded then tucked a strand of her hair behind her ear with his other hand. "Then Kade, most likely, will perform a mating ceremony when we're both ready." He swallowed hard. "It might be best to do that once Jesse and I are fully Redwoods, rather than confusing the Talon issue." It broke something inside him to say that, but he knew the Brentwoods and the rest of the Talons would eventually be okay with his decision. It wasn't as though there was another one to make.

Some people might have thought he'd be the one to stay within his Pack because he was the male, but those people were idiots. Gina was the one with the fated position, the one with the bond to her Pack that would eventually lead to even more strength and dominance. He would find a way to fit in because he had to. There was no way he'd make her give up her Pack when she was giving up everything else.

Maybe she's not giving up everything. Maybe she could be happy with you.

That small voice in his head startled him, but he pushed it away. He didn't need those kinds of thoughts.

"Are you sure you're ready to leave the Talons?" she asked.

He nodded. "For Jesse…and for you, yes I am."

Her eyes widened, and she smiled. Just a small smile, but he felt as if it was the largest of victories.

"And it's not like I'm leaving my Pack behind in all ways," he added. "The Talons and Redwoods are forming even more of a unit than they had before. That's why we have the council." That's why they had met.

She nodded. "We can talk about all of that once we make more plans," she said. "I think…I think…" She didn't finish her sentence. Instead, she wrapped her arm around his neck and pulled him toward her. Her lips pressed against his, and he lowered his head, leaning into the kiss.

His wolf whimpered, begging for more. He cupped her face fully then slanted his mouth over hers. She opened for him and tentatively touched her tongue to his. He growled then deepened the kiss.

She tasted of stir-fry and sweetness, and he craved more. He forced himself not to dwell on what would happen next. If he did, he'd pull away and run like the coward he was. He knew she'd never love him; she couldn't, not when he'd pushed her away like he had that first time.

He wouldn't allow himself to love her. He couldn't risk it.

Again, he pushed those thoughts away and focused on the woman in his arms. They might not have the mating wolves dreamed about, but he refused to ruin everything in the meaning of this moment. Gina deserved better.

He pulled away then rested his forehead against hers. "You taste amazing," he said softly.

"Don't use the pretty words you don't mean," she said, her voice cracking.

Annoyed, he pinched her chin and forced her gaze to his. He felt her wolf rise, buck at his challenge, but she didn't pull away. "I'm not going to lie to you. We're both being honest about *why* we're doing this, but I'm not going to allow you to be hurt any more than you are. I won't lie about what is happening, what I need, what I crave. I expect you to do the same. We have centuries together, and I'm not about to make you suffer during them."

She searched his face then nodded. "Fine," she said softly.

Good enough. He nodded then crushed his mouth to hers. She yelped then sank into him. He tangled his hand in her hair, gripping it so he could take control. She pushed against him, biting his lip.

"I'm not a submissive wolf, Quinn," she panted. "You don't get to take control."

He grinned then, his wolf coming to the surface. "Good. I want you to push back. I don't need you on your knees unless you want to be. The thought of you on your knees when I pump into you from behind turns me on though. When I fuck your mouth or your pussy, I want you to be right there with me. I want your hands on my body, your nails scoring my back. I want you to fuck me as hard as I fuck you. Sound good?"

Her pupils dilated, and she bit her lip. He leaned down and licked the spot she'd bitten, wanting a taste.

"You're going all in, aren't you?"

He kissed up her jaw then licked her earlobe. "I'm in this for the long haul." With his body and his soul. He had no choice in the matter, and if he thought about it hard enough, he knew he didn't want the choice. His heart, though, that would have to be hidden from her. He couldn't risk losing himself again when Gina thought more about what she was doing.

He didn't know if he could survive that.

Because while he'd loved Helena with the heart of a young man, Gina was turning out to be everything he wanted in a wolf.

That was dangerous.

"Then fuck me," she said. "Mate with me."

He put his hands on her ass then lifted her up. Her legs went around his waist, and his cock pressed against her heat. "Yes."

She kissed him while cupping his face. He nipped at her then kissed her back, all the while carrying her back to his bedroom.

He'd never brought a woman to his room. Helena hadn't lived here since he'd moved out of his place as soon as he could. It had been five long years since he'd been buried within a woman, and now he was starting to feel a bit nervous. Honestly, with the way Gina was wrapped around him, he wasn't sure how long he'd last.

He set her down at the foot of the bed then cupped her face before kissing her again, this time a bit rougher.

Her wolf was at the surface, and her eyes glowed gold. They both knew what was about to happen, and a small part of him was excited. That part *wanted* her. *All* of her.

He had to push that part away for its own good.

At least that's what he told himself.

Then he slammed his mind down from thinking and focused only on the woman in front of him. The gorgeous woman in front of him.

He stood back then stripped off his shirt. She let out a gasp then hesitantly put her hand out before pulling back. He took her hand in his then put her palm over his heart.

"It's okay, you can touch. You can do anything you want."

He watched her throat work as she swallowed hard then willed his cock to behave as she traced his chest with her fingertips. Her fingers danced along the ink on his arms and chest, seemingly taking in every inch of him. He let her explore, let her set the pace. If he didn't, he'd have her on her back and open for him in the blink of an eye.

"When did you get this?" she asked, her hands on his ink.

He cleared his throat. "When I was eighteen. I thought it was cool despite the fact I didn't really think about how long I'd have it." Considering wolves lived for centuries, that was a long freaking time.

"I like the fact that it's a wolf, yet not really. It's all tribal and lines."

He nodded then took a deep breath before putting his hand on her waist. Her gaze shot to his, and then she smiled.

His wolf perked up, wanting her to smile again.

His hands traced her hips then he gripped the edge of her shirt before pulling it over her head. He'd seen her naked before when they'd shifted, but now it was a whole different matter. Now he could rake his gaze over her body and learn every inch of her. She was his to bond with, his to make love to, his to learn and lick and taste.

She licked her lips, and he kissed her. They pressed their bodies against one another, only parting to strip off the rest of their clothes.

Soon they were naked, his cock hard, throbbing, and pressing into her belly. Her nipples pebbled against his skin, and he wanted a taste.

He knelt down before her then looked up. "I want to taste every inch of you before I fuck you, Gina."

She ran her hand over his head then gripped his hair. "More licking. Less talking."

He grinned, surprised, and then spread her thighs. She gasped when he licked her pussy in one long stroke. She was pink, wet, and ready, but he wanted to taste her on his tongue and have her come before he filled her.

She was seriously one beautiful wolf.

One beautiful witch.

Maybe if he told her that, she'd believe him.

One day.

He gripped her ass and spread her cheeks so he could get a better angle at her core. Her hand in his hair tightened, and he bit down on her clit, his face buried between her legs.

He lapped her up, his body craving her.

"Quinn!"

He bit down on her clit again, and she stiffened before she came. He kept sucking and licking, wanting to take her to the next crest. He wanted her to come over and over until she was nothing but a pile of sweaty Gina, content and mated. It was the wolf in him, and the bastard of a man as well.

When the tremors stopped, he stood up and took her mouth, wanting her taste on his lips. He already had her cream; now he wanted her tongue.

"I love your taste, Gina," he growled out. He was being honest, just like he said he'd be. If it left him open, then he'd deal with the consequences. "I'm going to want that pretty mouth of yours on my cock, but not right now."

She licked her lips then smiled. "Eager much?"

He nodded. "I'm not going to last long since it's been five years and I'd rather come for the first time in you, not down your throat."

Her eyes widened. "Five years? I forgot you said something like that."

He shrugged. "I didn't want anyone after Helena left."

Some of the light left her eyes, and he cursed.

"I didn't want anyone *before* you, Gina."

She shook her head. "Don't lie to try and make me feel better,

Quinn."

He could still taste her on his tongue, and yet he was already fucking this up. He cupped her face then kissed her hard. "I want you. Not anyone else. I didn't want to sleep with anyone else before because they weren't worth it. I'd lost my soul, and I didn't want to risk it again."

"Yet you're here with me to save your son, not because you want me. I get that. You don't have to pretty it up."

"Shit. I'm doing this wrong. I'm always doing things wrong with you. I want you. I wanted you the first time I saw you. That's why I was an asshole that day and the rest of the days since. I don't know what the future holds, and I know we're going about this backwards, but know that none of this is on you."

"But you said—"

He kissed her again to cut her off. "What I said before about you being a witch? I was wrong. I pushed you away to protect myself, and I hurt you in the process. I'm so sorry about that. You're a witch. I got that. You're going to be my witch." Her eyes widened at that, and honestly he surprised himself as well.

"Quinn…"

"We're going to talk about futures and what the next steps are later, I know, but I don't want you to lie beneath me, have me deep inside you, thinking I hate you. I don't, Gina. I can't."

Her eyes filled, and he sighed.

"I'm sorry I hurt you before. I'm so sorry."

Her fingers traced his ink again, and he closed his eyes. "I forgive you, Quinn. I don't know what you went through before, and honestly, I hope I never have to."

He met her gaze, and it felt like a boulder had been lifted from his shoulders. If he had any say about it, neither of them would go through it. He just had to trust her enough to make that happen. He was beginning to think he could.

"It's only you and me in this bed," he said softly, praying he was telling the truth. "Gina, you will be my mate, as I will be yours. Our souls will entwine, and we will be one, if only for a moment. There's no going back." He swallowed. "And I don't want to go back."

Now that he had her here, in his room, his bed, his arms, he knew he couldn't let her go.

That scared him more than he thought possible.

She tilted her head. "I'm standing here naked with you. I don't want to go back either. We'll talk about everything later, I promise. Now,

Quinn, please, fill me. I don't want to lose whatever moment we have left."

He licked his lips then kissed her again, knowing that they'd find a way to make this work. They had to.

His hands molded her ass while her hands roamed his back. Craving her, he lifted her up and then onto the bed. They fell together in a tangle of limbs, his legs giving out with his need.

He leaned up and grinned at the laughter in her eyes.

"Smooth," she teased.

"I'll show you smooth, witch, " he growled back. This time when he said the word "witch," it felt like an endearment, not a curse. That was progress at least.

He crushed his mouth to hers, rocking his body along hers. She arched up against him, her hands gripping his biceps. He pulled back, wanting more of her. When she licked her lips, he did the same then went to her breasts, sucking and nipping at her nipples.

"You have fantastic tits," he murmured then bit down.

She gasped then moaned, pressing her breasts into his face. With his free hand, he rolled her other nipple between his fingers then pinched.

"Oh, that feels so good," she panted.

He laved at her skin then switched to her other breast, wanting her eager and writhing beneath him. It had been so long since he'd been with a woman, but from the way Gina was reacting, maybe he hadn't lost his touch.

Or maybe it was just Gina…

"Please, I need to come, Quinn. I just need you."

He pulled his attention from her chest then kissed her again. When he leaned over her, he positioned himself at her entrance.

"You ready?" he asked, his voice a growl.

She blinked up at him. "Yes."

There was no hesitation, no worry in her voice.

Thank the goddess.

He slowly breached her entrance, keeping his gaze on hers. Her pussy tightened around his cock, her inner walls so damn tight he had to focus hard so he wouldn't come before he was fully inside her.

Since he was over her body on his forearms, she reached out and grasped his hand, and he sucked in a breath. Their fingers tangled then he cupped her face with his other hand.

If she let him touch her again, he'd go hard and sweaty next time. Right then, he only wanted to feel her around him as he bound their souls and their wolves.

Finally, sweet finally, he was inside her to the hilt.

"I need a second," he ground out, his body pulsing.

"You're really freaking big, Quinn," she panted. "Move. Please, for the love of the goddess, move."

He grinned before kissing her. "You say such sweet things." Then he moved, pulling out of her then slowly inching back in. The sweet torture would surely kill him, but he didn't care.

He was taking her future away and binding her to him. He'd make sure it would be worth it. There could be no other outcome.

"Faster!"

He shook his head. "Next time," he rasped out.

She froze then lifted her hips. "Next time," she repeated.

He pumped in and out of her slowly, watching her eyes darken as she rose over the crest. Right when he was about to come, she tilted her head and bared her neck.

"Mark me," she whispered.

His fangs lengthened, and he growled before lowering his head at the perfect angle so she could mark him as well. He never quit moving, never quit remembering that he was deep inside the woman fate had chosen for him despite his rejection.

He scored her neck before taking a deep breath.

"Quinn. Just do it. Please."

He licked the part of her neck that met her shoulder then closed his eyes. When he bit down, sliding through the skin, he shook. His wolf howled, rejoicing in the bond forming. He thrust his cock twice more within her before he came, her inner walls clenching around him as she did the same. He turned his head to the side, letting Gina mark him as hers. Her fangs slid into him, the pain nothing compared to the sweet ecstasy roaring through him.

The bond between them snapped into place so hard he felt as though he would break. It wove around their souls like a fire burst before flaring like a golden thread, unbending, unbroken.

The spot in his heart that had been dead, so cold for so long, warmed and filled with the essence that was all Gina. His wolf howled, practically prancing at the thought of Gina's wolf forever in his life.

He pulled his mouth away from her then licked the wound closed, his body shaking. When he moved to look into her eyes, he knew he'd never be the same.

Tears marked her cheeks, and she paled at the sight of him. When he moved to brush them away, she turned from him, leaving him wanting…yet not empty.

No, he'd never be empty again, not with Gina as his mate.

She'd mated with him for Jesse, yet it was Quinn who had come out ahead.

Their lives were forever connected, yet he didn't deserve it. She'd given up everything she could have had with another mate, and yet he could offer her nothing but his bond and promise to try not to hurt her again.

He didn't deserve Gina.

He didn't deserve anything.

Chapter Nine

Gina took two steps into her new home on Redwood Pack land and didn't feel the urge to run away. That was something, at least.

It had been two weeks since she'd mated with Quinn, and she still didn't know what she was doing. Sure, she saw him every day, but it wasn't like they talked about how they were feeling.

How was she supposed to do that when she didn't know what she was feeling herself? On one hand, she hated the fact that they'd both only mated to protect a boy who couldn't protect himself.

On the other, she couldn't help but want the man who had taken her and bonded with her. When she looked under the layers of hurt and pain, she saw the man he had once been, or at least the man she could admire and crave now. He wasn't a bad man, a bad wolf. No, he was loyal, fierce, and innately stoic. Yet those outer layers had hurt her and prevented him from ever feeling for her the want she needed in a true bond.

She was just so freaking confused, yet she couldn't stop and think about it. There was too much to do. The council had come back together, and while they tried to ignore the fact that their leaders were now mated, it was hard to do.

She and Quinn hadn't told anyone *why* they had mated, and most people thought it was because they wanted to, because they loved one another, not because of the true reason. Only her family and Quinn's friends had guessed, but she hadn't told them the truth.

She didn't want people to judge her or even Jesse for her decision. After all, she'd mated for the life of Jesse, not for love. She'd been the one to make it, so now she was the one who was going to have to live with it.

The council was working hard with the maternals and sentries to make their plans for having the two Packs work together actually happen. Gina hoped everything worked out and that the moon goddess gave them a break, but she honestly didn't know anymore.

It didn't help that she had no idea what to say to Quinn. They talked work, Pack issues, and Jesse, but that was it. They didn't talk about feelings or emotions, but she didn't think they could yet. Their bond was still too fresh, too new. She could feel him on the other side of the bond as well as her wolf could, and it scared her. If she looked too closely, she might get burned, and she couldn't afford that.

So, the council was well on its way to hopefully being helpful, she and Quinn were studiously avoiding talking about big issues, and thankfully, Jesse seemed to be getting better.

She ran a hand over her heart and let out a breath. That little pup was already turning out to be the light of her life. He'd accepted her as Quinn's mate surprisingly fast. He was still a little shy around her and called her Gina, but it was more than she could have ever asked for. They were learning each other much like she and Quinn were learning each other. In fact, Quinn and Jesse were coming over to the den later that day so they could all bond. Or at least try to. It was weird going about things so differently than most wolves, but she would find a way to make it work.

At least Jesse was getting better. He didn't have that much more energy than he had before, but between the bond and what Hannah and Walker had done, he wasn't getting tired like he used to. She hoped that meant he was well on the way to being mended.

She didn't live with them, but she *did* see Quinn and Jesse daily. It was hard to see them and not fall in love with them. That was one thing she promised herself she wouldn't do, yet she knew that might be futile.

She was bonded to that family, and now she was going to start bringing that family into her den. Her plans for moving in with Brie were over because she was a newly mated woman now who needed a place of her own. When Jesse was ready, he and Quinn would become Redwoods and move in with her. She hadn't wanted to bring them over now because Jesse needed to be at full strength before he cut his bond with his Alpha, and she didn't want to live with them among the Talons because she wasn't a Pack member.

It was all really confusing, and honestly, she felt like nothing was ever going to be okay again if she thought about it too hard.

She'd given up a chance at happiness, at least that's what Quinn had told her. Did she really believe that though? Would she have ever found another mate? Some wolves *never* found mates and were forced to find other ways of making a mating bond or a future. She had a mate. One that fate had picked. It was just that Quinn hadn't wanted her...at first.

Now he seemed to be okay with her bloodline and who she was, but she couldn't trust that, could she? See? So confusing. One day it would all make sense because if it didn't, she wasn't sure how she'd be able to function. As it was, she knew she wasn't at full speed.

Others gave her the benefit of the doubt because she was newly mated, but that wasn't it. She wasn't tired because she was up all night having glorious sex with Quinn. No, she was tired because she couldn't sleep since he *wasn't* there. They didn't even sleep under the same roof. In fact, other than that first night, she and Quinn hadn't made love again. She knew he was giving her space, but now she felt unwanted.

Again.

Apparently, her wolf and her brain were going crazy because she honestly didn't know what to do next beyond trying to make it through the day.

The first step would be to make her new, small house on the Redwood Pack land her home.

Their home.

She just hoped she was making the right choices because there was no turning back now.

When she'd told her parents that she was ready to move out, both of them looked like they wanted to say something but had held back. They weren't pushing her out, but they wanted to keep her safe somehow. She knew they were worried about her, but there was nothing she could do. Instead, they helped her find a small cottage on the edge of the Jamenson area of the den and let her live her life. The fact that they supported her and helped her when she needed it meant more to her than them voicing their concerns. They had the same ones as she did, so there was no point in worrying over things she couldn't change.

Finn and her dad had helped her move in some of the antique furniture they had in their storage units. Some had belonged to her grandparents while other pieces had belonged to her birth parents. It hurt deep down inside that neither set was alive, thanks to the war, but now she had a piece of them in this new world she wove.

Quinn and Jesse would be there in about half an hour to see the new place and have a meal. They were all trying, so that had to count for something. She just hated being in a state of flux. Not having her footing made her feel as if she was constantly trying to figure out what to do next, but things would settle down soon. The Pack was working with the Talons and with her and Quinn's mating, things would only get better on that front. Jesse would one day be fully healed, if the way he was slowly getting better was any indication.

Only her mating with Quinn was the truly scary thing.

Well, that and the fact that those bastards who'd cornered her on neutral land still gave her wary looks, as if she'd turn green and cackle like a Hollywood witch or something.

They had been punished by her father for attacking—or at least trying to attack—without cause, but they were still resentful. She just hoped they didn't do anything stupid. She honestly didn't have the energy to deal with the insecurities of a few wolves that didn't understand her powers. Okay, fine, she didn't understand them fully either, but she was learning. She was going to her Aunt Hannah weekly to learn to center. She'd even helped Jesse with his illness using her powers.

She wasn't a weak, unskilled witch.

She was learning.

Tired of her rambling thoughts, she ran her hand through her hair then walked out to her front yard. Quinn and Jesse would be there soon, and she didn't really want to start decorating or putting anything out until they lived with her. It seemed odd to do so without them since this would soon be *their* place. The fact that she'd picked it without them was weird enough.

The scent of two familiar, unwanted wolves reached her nostrils, and she planted her feet while trying to look casual. Two of the wolves who had tried to attack her with the Talons were prowling toward her in human from. The glares on their faces didn't bode well.

Damn it, she did *not* have time for this, and she didn't want Jesse to see anything that might happen if she had to use her wolf or her powers to get out of the situation. He might be a pup, but he was going to be *her* pup. She'd protect him with everything she had—even herself.

"What can I do for you boys?" she asked, her voice smooth. She wouldn't put her wolf up front unless she had to. No use beating these boys down until they made the first move.

"We just want to welcome you to your new home," the first wolf sneered.

"Yeah, then say get out. You should have gone to live with your new Talon mate," the other one said.

She raised a brow. "I don't think so, boys. I'm going to be the

Enforcer, in case you've forgotten. I'm a Redwood. Quinn will be one soon as well."

"You should have gone to your man and joined his Pack. What kind of pussy is this Quinn if he's letting his woman lead?"

She let out a breath. She hated ignorant fools. Every Pack had them. Even though most of the Redwoods and Talons were good and reasonable, some weren't. It was just the way of every community.

"You know what? I'm going to be nice and let you two walk out of here on your own two feet. I'm not in the mood to kick your asses today."

The first wolf snorted. "Like you could, *witch*."

That did it. Fuck him. Fuck all of them. She held out her palms and let her magic roll through her. It felt like a warm spark tingling through her system, but not an unpleasant one. No, this one was like she was waking up after a long sleep, eager to get on with her day. She'd been practicing so hard, and now it felt like things were actually working in her favor. Twin flames danced in her palms, and she growled at each of the wolves in front of her.

"I'm a witch. I'm a wolf. I'm blessed by the moon goddess to one day be the Enforcer. I know I will need to prove myself to you. I've been doing that since the day I first growled and shifted. You don't like my past, my blood, or who I am? That's fine. I can't change that. But no matter what your opinions of me are, you will learn to respect me or deal with the consequences. I have shown both of you that my wolf is more dominant. If you can't understand that, then we have a problem."

The weaker wolf in front of her knelt low to the ground, his body quivering. The other wolf, however, was a freaking idiot. He snarled then pounced. Without a second thought, she closed her hands, putting out the flames, and then pivoted so the wolf hit the ground instead of her. His face hit the dirt, and she picked him up by his neck then slammed him back into the ground, this time on his back. She straddled him and growled.

His wolf whimpered, but she was tired of this.

Tired of fighting for what she had because others wanted it, too.

"Are you finished? You are a strong wolf. I get that. But you are *not* stronger than me. Fighting within the Pack will only hurt us when it comes to outsiders. Don't you get that? You're *hurting* the Redwoods because of your prejudices. I'm done dealing with your shit. Get over yourself and learn your place. Respect who we are."

The wolf met her eyes for only a moment then lowered his own, defeated.

Her own wolf howled. She hadn't drawn a single drop of blood, and she had a feeling she'd resolved at least some of the issues going on in her Pack. It took power, not carnage, to do so.

Thank the goddess.

With one last look at the wolf below her, she stood up and glared. Both of the wolves ran in the other direction. If they'd been in wolf form, their tails would have been tucked between their legs. She knew proving her dominance would never be over—that was the way of the wolves—but she hoped this would put a damper on the whole prejudice thing. She'd had full control of her powers and hadn't used them to hurt another member of her Pack. That was something others who didn't know her worried about, and now she had proof she could handle things on her own.

"You were magnificent."

She jumped at Quinn's words then looked up to see him with Jesse in his arms walking toward her. Her mate had a frown on his face but still looked proud.

Warmth filled her at that look, but she pushed it down. She couldn't fall in love with him, she reminded herself.

"Are the bad wolves gone?" Jesse asked, and she smiled at the little boy in Quinn's arms. The two of them reached her and stood only a few inches away. She could scent their wolves, all warmth and forest, and the connection that proved she was theirs, at least as far as she would let them be.

She hesitantly reached out and cupped his little face. He grinned and rubbed against her skin. Her own wolf nudged at her, wanting to make sure this little pup knew he would always be taken care of.

She'd been adopted into a loving family and had never once thought she wasn't loved. She would make sure Jesse knew the same feelings—despite what went on between her and his father.

"Yes, they're gone. They just needed a little lesson. Don't worry, though, okay?"

"Okay." His eyes brightened as he looked behind her. "Is that our new home?"

She met Quinn's eyes, and he nodded at her. "Yes, when you're strong enough to go through bond changes, then you'll move in here with me." Her voice trembled a bit, and she had a feeling Quinn caught it.

It was a scary prospect. One day she'd been a wolf just finding her place within the Pack, and the next she was a stepmother to a sick pup and mated to a wolf who would never love her.

She'd deal though. She always did.

"Can I see inside?" he asked, then grinned at her. Jesse had the best smile, and he knew it. He was going to be trouble when he got older, and she couldn't wait. The fact that he would be able to get older at all made everything worthwhile.

"Come on then," she said and held back a gasp when he wrapped his arm around her neck. She stepped closer to him and Quinn handed him over, making sure she had him tucked close. He was five, so he was already too big to be held most days, but she was a wolf and could handle it. Plus, this was a new place so she understood he wanted the comfort.

She met Quinn's eyes, and he gave her an odd look then moved toward the house. "This is it. It's an older cottage that's been in my family for a while now. It has enough land that if we want to build on, we can."

"It's great, Gina. Perfect."

She looked over at Quinn and smiled softly. "Thanks. I've only spent a couple of nights in it and haven't unpacked really. I was just waiting...you know."

He met her gaze and nodded. "I get it. Soon, I think."

Her heart raced, and she sucked in a breath. Technically, with the bond between them already working, they didn't have to live together. Yes, the two would have to join her Pack because of the ways the other Pack bonds and wards worked, but they didn't have to act like a mated couple if they didn't want to. It would be awkward and horrible, but she could deal with it. But Quinn was doing everything in his power to show her that he could be a normal mate. He was going to become a Redwood, live with her, and raise his son with her.

He just didn't love her.

She didn't need that though. And if she told herself that enough times, maybe she'd believe it.

"Well, come on in, I'll give you a tour."

"Are you sleeping here all alone?" Jesse asked when she set him down.

"Yes. For now. Want to see your room? I don't have anything in it yet since I figured you'd want your own things."

"Okay, I like that. But I think you should come home with us. That way you're not alone. Being alone is sad."

Tears pricked at her eyes, and she shook her head. "You and your Dad need to stay at your place so you can finish getting better. I'll be here when you're ready."

Jesse stopped his perusal of the house and turned toward her. "But you're all alone. Can't you stay with us for one night? That way you aren't sad anymore?"

She swallowed hard and opened her mouth to say something, but Quinn stepped in.

"I think that's a great idea, Gina," he said, his voice low. "That will give us some time to get to know one another."

She searched his face, wondering what the hell he was thinking. She didn't know if she could do this. She might have been strong, but she wasn't sure she could handle being near him and not falling for him.

How was she going to do it when he was living with her?

"Just one night, Gina," he said softly. "Just to see."

If she could handle one night with him and not fall, she'd be okay. She could do this. She could find a way to make it work. That balance between heaven and hell was right at her fingertips. She just had to find a way to make it work.

"Okay. Let me pack a bag."

Approval shone in Quinn's eyes, and he smiled. "Sounds good to me."

"Yay!" Jesse rushed at her and grabbed her legs in a hug. "I can't wait. I love sleepovers."

She ran a hand over his head. Sleepovers…with Quinn.

Oh, boy. This was going to be her own personal hell.

She'd make it work though. She'd chosen her fate. Now she had to live with it.

* * * *

"You're kidding," Quinn said on a laugh. He took a sip of his beer and shook his head. "How long did it take Finn to figure it out?"

"Well, the smell got pretty bad after a week. He found the moldy cheese in his closet soon after." Gina grinned. "He wasn't happy, but hello, he told Matt that I had a crush on him, so I had to get back at him somehow."

He snorted then shook his head. After Jesse had invited Gina over to stay the night, they'd quickly packed her a bag and headed back to the Talon den. He'd done his best to make sure she felt comfortable, but he wasn't sure how she was doing. They spent a few hours together each day, but other than the fact that Jesse treated her more warmly than he had before—which was saying something since the kid had latched onto her quickly—they hadn't really done anything differently.

Seeing her in the home she'd chosen for them had shocked him. He'd known it was coming and had given her the reins since he hadn't been able to do anything else for her. The home, however, felt like he could have moved right it. It wasn't huge but had a warm feeling that pulled at him, even if nothing was truly unpacked. He liked the fact that she was waiting for him to do the rest. It was as if she wanted to make sure they were part of it. It wasn't just them moving into her home. It was the three of them moving into *their* home.

Things sure changed fast as hell, but he was beginning to find his footing. Telling the Talons that he was leaving had almost killed him, but they'd been supportive. They understood the sacrifice Gina had made and hadn't judged them for it. Or at least, he hadn't caught on to it. He'd always hold the Talons in his heart. They were the Pack of his family, his ancestors, his son, but he wouldn't go into the Redwoods without them knowing he'd be handing over his allegiance.

It wasn't an easy decision, but it was something he had to do. He at least had that much honor left.

"You're really close to your brothers then," he said, bringing his focus back to the matter at hand. He wanted to get to know Gina. It scared him how much. He might have gone into his mating, this partnership, thinking he would hide himself from her, but he didn't know how much longer he could do that. The mating bond pulsed between them, bringing him closer to her, even as he tried to deny it.

He wasn't sure what was coming or even how they would travel the path they'd made for themselves, but he knew he couldn't go on trying to act like he wasn't affected. His wolf wanted her; *he* wanted her.

Could he one day love her?

If he could let go and face the chance of pain, yes, yes he could. She was strong, worthy, funny, brilliant, and beautiful. Everything he wanted in a mate. Or at least, everything he thought he'd wanted in a mate before he'd met Helena.

Helena had been striking. She had been one of the most beautiful women in the entire den. He'd liked the way she'd laugh or try to joke around more than anything. She didn't take much seriously, which he'd thought had helped him calm down after a shift or long day spent dealing with wolves who tried to prove their dominance to him. The Pack had been much different before Gideon took over, and the transition had not been easy. Coming home to Helena had been nice because she just wanted to play or have sex. Easy.

Then she'd gotten pregnant, and things turned to shit.

Now that he thought about what he wanted, he knew it wasn't a woman like Helena. Yeah, she was beautiful, but looks only went so far.

He didn't like comparing Gina to her, but he couldn't help it.

Gina wasn't the same kind of beauty as Helena. While Helena was all ice and Nordic features, Gina was warmth and strength wrapped up in a sultry aura. She also was much more dominant than Helena had ever been. The way she fought back and fought for herself turned him on more than he'd thought possible.

He liked that, while he could protect her if needed, she was just as capable of protecting herself. He hadn't known he'd wanted that until she'd shown up in his life.

And now they were mates, and she wasn't going away. Not that he wanted her to.

His mind whirled.

He didn't want her to go.

He wanted her to stay.

What the hell had happened in these short days since they'd been mated?

He'd seen the true side of her courage and had finally, what? Said it was okay to risk being hurt again? He wasn't sure, but he knew he couldn't hurt Gina in the process. He couldn't be the asshole he'd been. Not when she'd done nothing wrong but been herself.

"Quinn? You aren't listening to me. What's going on?"

He shook his head and cleared his thoughts. "I'm just thinking. It's not a big deal."

She frowned. "Thinking about what? You looked really serious just then, like someone had sucked the air out of the room."

He set his beer down then cupped her face. Her eyes widened, but she didn't move away. Progress.

"Thank you," he whispered.

She closed her eyes. "Don't thank me, please."

Quinn lowered his head so he was only a whisper away from her lips. "I have to. Thank you for taking a chance on us. I...I like you. I admire you. I want to know you more. Do you think you'll let me do that?"

She opened her eyes and sucked in a breath. He could feel the heat of her skin on his, but he didn't move. He couldn't.

"I want to know you, too."

He growled softly then took her lips in a kiss.

She moaned under him, and he brushed his tongue against hers, deepening the kiss. She tasted of sweetness and promise, and he wanted more of her. Craved more.

She shifted and ended up on his lap, her core right above his dick. He groaned then pulled back, trying to catch his breath.

"I actually wanted to talk," he said on a laugh. "You know, find out who you are beyond the blessed Redwood wolf and witch."

She cupped his face and grinned. "I want to know you beyond the father and scarred wolf that everyone sees." She swallowed hard. "I had thought you wanted nothing to do with that when I came here before."

He would regret that day until he died. He'd acted rashly and might have ruined a chance at healing, at a future. That was, if he could make this work with Gina. Hope never worked without the inherent risk, and he knew he had to be prepared to make that happen.

He brushed her hair away from her face. "I think we went about this the wrong way, and we should start over."

Her eyes widened. "Uh, Quinn? We're already mated. Your son is sleeping in the room behind us, and I'm currently straddling your legs. I mean, I can feel your cock under me so I know you're not unaffected."

He let out a hoarse chuckle. "Damn right I'm not unaffected. What I'm saying is, we should look at what we're doing and what we have in front of us without worrying about what happened before."

Her jaw dropped. "You...you're serious?"

"I think..."

He didn't get a chance to say what he was going to. Instead, his wolf went on alert as the scent of someone who should not have been anywhere close to him invaded his senses.

Gina stiffened. "Quinn? What's wrong?"

His eyes widened then he looked toward the front door as the one person he never wanted to see again walked through.

"Helena," he growled.

Gina sucked in a breath but didn't move.

Helena grinned at him, her bright blue eyes filled with something he couldn't decipher, and her long blonde hair blowing in the breeze.

"Quinn. I'm back."

Hell. No.

She couldn't be back. He wouldn't have her back.

Fate really fucking hated him.

Hated. Him.

Chapter Ten

Gina slowly slid off Quinn's lap, her body tight as a string. She refused to look at him because, if she did, she was afraid of what she'd see. Plus, she needed to keep her eyes on the wolf that had walked through the door.

Helena.

Quinn's mate.

In his home.

What. The. Hell.

Her wolf whimpered then thought better and growled.

She didn't say anything.

She couldn't.

Instead, she stood there like a freaking idiot and watched the woman that Quinn had once loved—or maybe *still* loved—walk through the door like she owned the place. She knew Helena had never lived here, but that didn't stop the woman from acting like she belonged.

Belonged while Gina didn't.

Holy hell, there wasn't a guidebook for this. She had no idea what to do. From the look on Quinn's face, he didn't either. That hurt her more than it should have. If he'd truly hated Helena like he said he had, he'd have done something by now. Yelled or thrown her out.

Instead, they were standing there like they had something to say yet didn't know how to say it, and Gina was breaking.

Again.

This was the woman who Quinn had chosen. The one he'd put his heart and soul into loving. Gina was the woman he'd been forced to be with. Helena was Jesse's mother. Gina was nothing.

She wasn't sure she could handle much more. If things had been different, if Quinn had mated with her because he'd wanted to, not because he'd *had* to, maybe she'd have fought, but she couldn't.

Why bother?

Who was this wolf inside her who had given up? Who was this woman who wanted to run away and not deal with the fact that the woman who had broken Quinn's heart and left the Pack was now in Quinn's domain?

Gina didn't, and she didn't like who she was becoming.

She was a dominant wolf. She should fight for what she wanted.

Only she didn't know what she wanted...she didn't know what *Quinn* wanted. She might be mated to Quinn, but there was evidently a way to break the mating bond. If that's what Quinn wanted...

Bile rose in her mouth, yet still, she didn't speak. She couldn't be the one to do so. It had to be Quinn and Helena.

"What the hell are you doing here?" Quinn growled. His power swept through the room, and even Gina's knees buckled under its weight. The hair on her arms stood on end, and she was determined not to kneel under the strength of his wolf. She would *not* kneel in front of Helena.

The other woman whimpered then went to her knees, her head down as she bared her throat.

"Quinn...please forgive me."

Quinn's whole body shook, and Gina knew he was fighting for control. She didn't know what she should do, but she knew she couldn't let him tear Helena into small pieces—even though she wanted to do that herself. The other woman had almost killed Quinn and Jesse, the family she loved but shouldn't.

Helena deserved far worse than being torn into bits.

Yet she was Jesse's mother.

Quinn's love.

"Get out," Quinn snapped, and Gina shot her gaze to him, her heart pounding. Who? "Just get out. I don't know how you got through the wards or who helped you, but they will pay for it."

"Quinn. I'm so sorry. I just needed space, and I didn't know how to do it."

"Shut up!" he yelled. "I don't care. You need to leave before I kill you, and I won't have your blood on my hands. I won't do that to Jesse."

Helena looked up, tears in her eyes. "How *is* Jesse?"

The woman looked as if she actually cared about how her son was, but Gina couldn't take those words at face value. Helena had tainted his soul and *left*. That didn't give her the right to care about those she'd left behind. Yet Gina's mind still fought itself over what she should do, whether she should stay. Quinn clearly needed to talk to Helena and find out what had happened, and she wasn't sure he could do it with Gina in the room.

She didn't want to go…but maybe she should.

Her heart raced, and she let out a whimper of her own.

Quinn's gaze shot to hers. "Stay," he growled out, his eyes glowing gold. His wolf was right at the surface. This was one dangerous male, yet her wolf nudged at her, wanting his touch.

God, she didn't know what to do, and that annoyed her more than anything. She made decisions and kept to them. She didn't run away, and yet she felt as though she had to. This mating was killing her slowly, one inch at a time, and she didn't see a way out of it. Didn't see a way out of the pain beyond making sure Quinn and Jesse were happy.

Why did she have to be the better person? Why couldn't Quinn just love her and choose her?

Why did there have to be a choice?

"I should go," she whispered. "You need time."

He narrowed his eyes and shook his head. "Stay," he repeated.

"Quinn? Who is this? Why is there a woman in your house?"

Quinn roared. "Fuck you, Helena. You don't get to ask those questions." He turned back to Gina. "Don't go."

"Daddy? Gina?"

Gina's eyes widened, and she turned to Jesse, who stumbled his way into the room, his eyes half closed.

"Jesse," she whispered.

"Who's that, Gina?" he asked then put his hand in hers.

Her heart broke that much more.

"Jesse…" Helena breathed.

Quinn quickly stood in front of Jesse and Gina. "Get. Out." He flared his power again, and this time Gina was forced to her knees. She held Jesse close to her, and he burrowed into her body.

Gina heard Helena scramble away then Quinn's footsteps as he followed her. She held onto Jesse, rubbing his back, and flinched when Quinn slammed the door shut.

"Who was that?" Jesse asked, his voice shaking.

Gina pulled back and cupped his face. "I'm sorry we woke you." She wasn't about to tell him about Helena. That would be Quinn's job if he chose to do that.

Helena had technically lost all parental rights when she broke the mating bond. She had no right to Jesse or to even see him according to wolf laws. However, that didn't mean Jesse didn't deserve to know. This was all about the boy.

Everything Gina was doing was all about Jesse.

Jesse scrunched his face then shook his head. "You didn't answer me."

"That was no one," Quinn said calmly.

Surprised, Gina looked up at him.

He shook his head then knelt beside them. "It was no one important. Now, I'm sorry we woke you. Are you feeling okay?"

Jesse nodded then held out his arms. Quinn smiled slightly then picked Jesse up. "I'm going to put him back to bed," he said over his shoulder. "We need to talk."

She ran a hand over her face but didn't say anything. She honestly didn't know what to say at all.

He frowned at her, looked as though he wanted to say something else, and then turned with Jesse in his arms. Jesse waved, and she lifted her arm, waving slowly back. Her eyes burned, but she blinked the tears away. It wouldn't do any good to cry now. Her emotions were all over the place, and she wasn't sure what to think.

One moment she and Quinn were getting hot and heavy on the couch, actually talking about a future and what it meant for them to be mates, and the next the woman from his past walked through the door and Gina's dreams were shattered.

It didn't matter that Quinn had told Gina to stay while kicking Helena out.

Things weren't black and white, and nothing was ever that easy.

Gina had things to think about, and she wasn't sure she could do it with Quinn in the same room with her. Her heart was already hurt before she'd come over that night, and her head had already been so full of confusing thoughts she couldn't breathe.

Now she was at the point where if she worried about one more thing she would burst.

On shaky legs, she walked over to the notepad on the fridge and jotted down a note. It didn't say anything about what she was thinking or what she felt, because, honestly, she couldn't put any of that into words anyway.

Instead, she said she'd see him in the morning and that she was leaving. Not forever.

She hoped she was doing the right thing, but she wasn't sure. She wasn't sure about anything anymore.

As quietly as she could, she left the house and her mate behind and made her way to her car.

"Gina?"

She froze then looked over at Lorenzo, her fellow council member. He looked as if he was on a late-night run, and considering he was part of their security force, that made sense.

"Lorenzo," she said smoothly, surprised that her voice didn't break.

He frowned then looked between her and Quinn's home. "Why are you heading out in the middle of the night? Is everything okay?"

She nodded, burying the lie. "I'm just heading back to my den for the night."

He sighed. "It's going to suck losing Quinn to the Redwoods, but it's not like you guys are far away, you know? I'm just glad he finally has a chance to be happy."

She nodded and pasted a smile on her face. "I'm sorry he had to make that choice."

Lorenzo shrugged. "Well, it had to happen. It's not like we can have mated pairs across Pack lines. That would just lead to more issues than we can deal with. It used to happen all the time when the Talons were mating frequently." He smiled softly. "The fact that you and Quinn are mating at all is a miracle. A blessing from the moon goddess. I guess the council was a good idea after all."

She kept her smile up, but she knew her eyes held her pain. She couldn't help it. Lorenzo's smile fell, and he took a step forward.

"Damn. What's going on Gina?"

She shook her head. "I...I need to go back." She sucked in a breath, knowing she had to say something. "Tell Gideon Helena's back. Will you?" She knew Quinn would get to it, but with his attention on Jesse, it would take time. Plus Helena was crawling around the den right then, and Gina wasn't happy about that fact.

Lorenzo's eyes widened, and he cursed. "You've got to be kidding." He looked between her and Quinn's house again. "Gina. Don't go. Quinn needs you."

She took another step toward her car. "Just tell Gideon. Okay? I need to go back to my den."

"Gina."

"Please, Lorenzo. I can't...not tonight."

He sighed but didn't move forward. "I'm so goddamn sorry, Gina. Just because Helena is here, though, that doesn't mean you're not still mated to Quinn."

She looked over her shoulder and gave him a sad smile. "Doesn't it? I'm not sure about anything anymore. Good night, Lorenzo." With that, she got in her car and headed home.

Home to an empty house with packed-up boxes and nobody to welcome her when she stepped inside. It was a shell of a dream that might never happen.

She'd mated with Quinn to save his son and because, if she was honest with herself, she wanted the man. She'd done the stupid thing and fallen in love with him and the family they could have had.

She knew she shouldn't have done it, and now there was no way out.

She'd mated a man she shouldn't have loved, and now his past was back to bite her in the ass. Fate royally sucked.

* * * *

She'd left him.

Quinn still couldn't believe Gina had just walked out of the house and hadn't said a word. He sighed and shook his head. No, sadly, he *could* believe that. He'd done nothing to show her that she should be with him. He'd only shown her the door and hurt her. Sure he'd been on the verge of trying to open up, but that meant nothing in the grand scheme of things.

He was an idiot, and now he had to pay the consequences. He'd been so scared about getting hurt again, he'd hurt the one person who had given up everything and asked for nothing in return.

He didn't deserve Gina, but now he'd make sure he did everything in his power to make it work. He might have been slow on the uptake, but there was no way he'd let Gina out of his grasp. She was good for his soul, good for his son, good for their Packs.

As soon as she came back to the den that afternoon, he'd talk with her and sort it all out. He didn't have another choice—not if he wanted to make things work between the two of them. They were mates, and he wasn't going to change that. He just prayed she didn't want to change things herself.

"You ready to go?" Gideon asked as he came up to his side.

"As ready as I'll ever be."

As soon as Quinn had found out Gina had left, he'd walked outside only to find Lorenzo standing there with a sad expression on his face. He said Gina had left, and he'd called ahead to make sure she made it out okay. Quinn could only be grateful that Lorenzo had thought to protect his mate when he couldn't. Lorenzo had also mentioned the fact that he'd called Gideon to tell him about Helena.

Quinn should have done it himself, but he'd been so out of his depth he'd focused on Gina and Jesse and not the very real problem that Helena was back, not only in the area but on Pack land.

Apparently an old friend of hers had let her in without alerting the Enforcer or anyone else in the Pack. That friend wouldn't be punished since, technically, he'd done nothing wrong. Helena hadn't been banished from Pack land. She'd simply left. Only there was nothing simple about it.

Now that the entire den knew Helena was back, they'd quickly rounded her up, and now there would be a Pack circle to decide what to do. She'd almost killed two Pack members when she'd escaped before and had broken her Alpha's trust by severing the bond.

There had to be repercussions. At least that's what Quinn hoped. What was interesting about all of this, though, was that Gideon hadn't been the one to call the Pack meeting. No, the elders had done it.

Quinn hadn't heard of another time that the elders had done such a thing, but he knew it had happened in other Packs. The elders had the power to call meetings, though the Alpha would be the one to lead it. The laws were written by the Alpha since his word *was* law, but the elders held sway as well. The fact that these particular elders were close to the former Alpha didn't sit well on Quinn's shoulders. There was nothing he could accomplish by worrying, however, so he'd go to the circle, find out what would happen to Helena, then find Gina and tell her he wanted a future.

All in a day's work.

"Do you know what you want the outcome to be?" Gideon asked, his voice low as not to carry.

Quinn frowned and looked at his Alpha and friend. "I want Helena out of my life forever. I don't want her near Jesse. She almost killed him. I want to forget Helena was ever part of my life and move on."

Gideon nodded. "With Gina."

"With Gina," he said without hesitation.

Gideon's eyes warmed. "That's a dramatic change from the way you acted before."

"I was impulsive before. I can't deny the pull I feel for her. If I'd seen her before all of this happened all those years ago, there wouldn't have been a second thought."

"That second thought hurt the hell out of her."

He flinched at his Alpha's words. "Yes. And I'm going to do my best to make it up to her."

"Do you love her?"

Quinn swallowed hard then let out a breath. "I...I think I could. It's too soon for me to say that. And when I do? It needs to be to her, not to someone else."

"Good for you, man. Good for you. Now, let's get this show on the road, and then we can deal with the other thousand things we have to do for the Pack and your mating bond."

Quinn groaned. "It's never-ending."

"Hey, at least you aren't Alpha."

"True. And thank the moon goddess for that."

Gideon flipped him off then prowled into the stone circle that acted as their Pack circle as well as mating circle in those times of need. It was the first thing that had been established when the Talons settled here all those years ago. The amount of magic that had been bled and beaten into the stones after centuries of ceremony and honor was staggering. No doubt the Redwood circle, which was slightly older, was even more magical.

He stepped into the circle then froze as a familiar scent reached his nose.

He turned and frowned. "Gina?"

She gave him a small wave but didn't smile. "Your elders called me personally to be here. I wasn't too pleased with a summons from a Pack not of my own, but if it's for you, I'll do it."

He reached out and cupped her face, pleased when she didn't back away. "You slay me, Gina."

She leaned into his hold but didn't stand on her toes to kiss him like she had before. "Don't say things like that. Please."

He shook his head then lowered his lips to hers. She didn't kiss him back, but she didn't lean away. That was something at least.

"You are remarkable. Will you stand by my side during this?" His wolf wanted her in his sight at all times, and the man didn't want to do this without her.

She looked pained but nodded. "Okay. Is Jesse with you?"

"No, he's with some of the maternals and other children. All of the Brentwoods had to be here, or he'd be with them." He let out a breath. "I don't want him to see Helena. I don't want him to hear the excuses she's bound to make."

"Quinn, she was your mate. Are you sure you can move past that? Because you didn't before."

He growled softly, but it was at himself, not her. "We will talk about the mistakes I've made with you and how I've treated you poorly once this is over. I will make it up to you, Gina. *Everything*. As for Helena? I don't want her."

Gina didn't look as though she believed him, and he knew he had a long journey in proving himself to her. After all, it had taken him far too long to realize that he wanted what fate had provided for him—Gina. And now he had to pay the price for that hesitation, for that denial. He'd do that readily as long as he got to have Gina by his side.

Only he didn't know if he deserved that. He'd just have to see.

"We're going to be late," she said softly then pulled away.

His wolf nudged at him, and he gripped her hand. She looked down at their clasped hands then up at him before turning back toward the stone entrance. They walked into the circle as a mated pair, and he prayed that it symbolized something more than just an easy walk.

There was no one in the center of the circle yet, but most of the Pack had taken their seats. The Brentwoods were in their royal box, with the elders on the other side of the circle in theirs. Quinn pulled Gina toward the Brentwood area and stopped directly beside it. He was a lieutenant, so it was his job to protect the Alpha. This circle was about him and his past. He needed to be close to the action.

"Let's begin," Gideon said when they were all seated. His voice boomed over the circle. That low growl that always seemed present in his Alpha's bass forced his wolf to pay attention.

"Yes, Gideon, let's begin." The elder leader, Shannon, glared at the Alpha as she spoke. The woman had never liked Gideon and his modern ways. Modern meant Gideon was less brutal and more fair, but that wasn't the point at the moment.

Shannon raised her chin and waved her arm. At that signal, Helena strode into the center of the circle. To anyone else, his former mate looked contrite, solemn. Yet Quinn knew her better than that. Or at least he thought he did. There was something off with the way she held herself, as if she was trying too hard to appear small. Helena wanted something, and it wasn't him or Jesse.

Most likely, it was Pack protection, and that annoyed him like no other. The years hadn't been kind to her. While she hadn't aged since she was a wolf, she had a few new scars and a frantic look about her that told him she hadn't had the time of her life like she'd wanted to outside the Talon wards.

Well, fuck her and everything she stood for. He wanted her out of his sight, but he had a feeling it wasn't going to be easy. It was never easy.

"You're not Pack, Helena," Gideon growled, and she flinched. "You made sure of that when you not only cut the connection between your mate and son, but you severed Pack ties."

Helena let her tears fall, yet Quinn felt nothing for her. He squeezed Gina's hand, trying to put his thoughts and feelings into that one motion. She didn't squeeze back.

"I made a mistake all those years ago," Helena said, her voice cracking.

Quinn growled but stopped when Gideon shot him a look.

"What was your mistake? Using dark magic to do something so taboo that no one has ever done it before or since? Or maybe it was almost killing Quinn because of your selfishness? Hmm? Oh, I know...it was when you almost killed your newborn baby because you couldn't handle it. Instead of coming to me or *any* of us, you ran away and broke away form the Pack. You betrayed us. You betrayed your son. You betrayed your mate. You betrayed yourself."

Quinn sucked in a breath at his Alpha's words. Damn, Gideon was pissed and yet was saying everything that had rolled through Quinn's head countless times.

"I'm sorry," Helena whimpered.

"She made a mistake, Gideon," Shannon crooned. "Every wolf is allowed to make a mistake. She wasn't banished back then, so it must not have been too bad."

Quinn's eyes boggled, and Gina squeezed his hand.

"I want my mate back," Helena said. "I want my son. I was out of my mind when I left, and now I know I've made mistakes, but I want my son and Quinn. The moon goddess blessed us, and I can't keep away from them any longer." She turned toward the rest of the Pack, pleading. "I'm a mother. Can't you see that? It was the witch who made me do what I did. It was her power. I'm a victim just like Quinn and Jesse." She fell to her knees, her cheeks stained with tears. "Please. Let me have my baby. Let me have my mate."

"Unbelievable," Quinn growled then pulled his gaze away from Helena to stare at Gina. "Don't believe her. She's lying."

Gina met his eyes and sighed. "A witch couldn't have taken the threat between your souls without Helena's free will. At least that's what I think, but she's here now, Quinn. Wouldn't she be better for Jesse in terms of the bond than me?"

Quinn growled and opened his mouth, but Shannon beat him to the punch.

"Quiet, Redwood," she snapped. "You're here to see the mate Quinn should have had. Don't you see that you're hurting a bond that came before you?"

"Back off," Quinn said, his voice low.

"Know your place, wolf," Shannon snapped.

"Quiet. All of you." Gideon raked his claws over the stone pillar in front of him, and Quinn held back a wince. The Alpha was pissed. "Gina and Quinn are mated now, Helena. You're too late. And even if you'd come earlier, you broke everything you could have had. It's over."

"Not so fast, Alpha," Shannon interrupted.

"Excuse me?" Gideon said, his voice a whip.

"Quinn mated both of them. This isn't a trinity bond or a full threesome or that would be one thing. No, this is unprecedented. Technically, the moon goddess chose both Gina and Helena. We need to see how this plays out."

"Fuck no," Quinn yelled. "I have a mate now. Fuck Helena and fuck whatever you think you're doing."

"Quinn," Gina whispered, pulling on his hand. "Don't yell at the elders."

"I'll yell at whoever I want to. They can't tell me who to mate."

Shannon smiled, and chills slid down his back. "Oh. I believe I can. Or at least I can provide the way. You see, since you've mated both of them, that's a sign of indecision. And you know what must happen when someone can't decide between two mates."

"You've got to be kidding me," Gideon snapped. "A mating circle? You want Gina and Helena to fight in a mating circle?"

Shannon nodded. "Yes. It's the way of the wolves. You can't change the laws, Alpha." She narrowed her eyes. "Though I know you've tried."

Quinn pulled Gina to his side, wrapping his arm around her. She didn't pull away. Instead, she put her arm around his waist. His wolf nudged at her, wanting to scent her and make sure everyone knew she was his.

"You can't make them fight," Quinn said, trying to keep calm. This couldn't be happening. This was ridiculous. "I'm *mated* to Gina. We have a bond. You can't force her to fight for me when she already has me."

Shannon shook her head. "We've never had a case like this before, meaning we must follow the laws that closely resemble it. Helena has a chance to be your mate, meaning she must fight for it. Bonds, as we've seen, can be broken when, I mean if, she wins."

Did the elder really hate the new generation of wolves enough that she wanted to break him again? What the hell was going on?

"Gideon. Do something."

His Alpha glared at Shannon then faced Quinn. "I can't make up new laws on the spot, Quinn. Since the elders are forcing a mating circle, then it will have to be done." He narrowed his eyes. "This will not be happening again though."

"Well, bully for the next person," he spat. "What about now? I'm not forcing her to fight for me."

"There's nothing I can do," Gideon whispered, looking for all the world as though the weight on his shoulders was too much to bear.

And what if she didn't fight?

What if she left him standing there and broke the bond? Not only would it break him if she left, but it could hurt Jesse as well.

Damn Helena.

Damn himself.

If Gina didn't fight for him, he'd lose everything...everything he hadn't known he wanted.

Chapter Eleven

Gina's pulse pounded in her ears, and she had to struggle to breathe. It didn't make any sense. *None* of this made any sense. She wasn't even a freaking Talon, and now she had to follow an elder's proclamation or risk losing the mating bond she'd just found in the first place.

Holy hell, what was she going to do?

Quinn put his hands on her hips and brought her back to his front. She shuddered out a breath, letting his scent wash over her. Her wolf was beyond in love with the wolf behind her and knew that they should be together through thick and thin.

The woman was more hesitant.

She'd had to be.

Quinn put his mouth to her ear, his breath sending warm shock waves down her body—soothing yet putting her near a new kind of edge.

"Let's get out of the circle and head back to my place. We can talk then."

She nodded but didn't turn, afraid that once she looked at him she'd give in and fight for a man who might not want her.

He led her to his home, ignoring people calling for them. She didn't want to talk to anyone but Quinn. She wasn't weak, but goddess, things kept piling up, and she didn't know how she was going to deal with it. She just needed to stop and think about every detail then lead with her mind, not with her heart.

If she could.

When they walked into his home, she relaxed marginally and pulled away.

"Gina."

She looked up at Quinn, at the sound of his deep voice. "Your former mate is a bitch." Her eyes widened at what slipped out, but she didn't regret it. She was done holding herself back. Done treading lightly to save someone else pain…to save herself pain. All it had done was put her in a position where she was going to be hurt anyway—emotionally *and* physically.

Quinn blinked then snorted. "Yeah. She is." He reached out and cupped her face. The calluses on his thumbs brushed her skin, and she shivered.

She loved this man.

Loved the way he protected what was his, loved the way he threw himself into everything he did. Loved the way he was as dominant as an Alpha, but stepped aside when he needed to.

He was a wolf that made her feel safe yet let her fight for herself at the same time.

She loved the man as well, not just the wolf. Quinn had done what he'd promised he'd never do—mate another. He was ready to willingly leave his Pack for her and his son.

She saw the nobility in that…even if she was scared that he wanted Helena back. It didn't make any sense, and it killed her that she was being so insecure, but she couldn't help it.

"What are you thinking about so hard, Gina?" he asked, his voice low.

She narrowed her eyes at him and pulled back. "What do you think? God, Quinn. Your elder wants me to fight for my life in a mating circle so I can have the right to mate you. I'm *already* mated to you. It doesn't make any sense."

Quinn growled low. "No. It doesn't. That bitch Shannon has a vendetta against Gideon and everyone associated with him. She's using every rule or half rule she can to find a way to hurt us. I'm so sorry you're being thrown in the middle of it."

"I…I don't know what I'm going to do," she whispered. It hurt that she couldn't just come out and say she wanted this mating. She was being a coward, and that's not how she was raised.

Melanie and Kade had been through a mating circle during their initial mating. Everything had turned out all right eventually. For a moment, she thought about calling her parents just to hear them, but stopped herself. This was between her and Quinn—and the rest of the Pack. She needed to learn to do things on her own—at least for now.

Quinn looked hurt for a moment then sighed. He took her hand in his and traced a finger along her palm. She shuddered a breath at the contact, wanting more. The mating urge between them rode her hard, and it clouded her thoughts. It didn't help that they hadn't made love since the first night. In fact, last night was the first time she'd truly felt as though he wanted something more...then Helena had shown up.

"I don't want you to do anything you don't want to do." He met her gaze, his finger still tracing her palm. "I already made you mate with me for Jesse when you didn't want to. I'm not going to do that again."

Her wolf growled, and she wanted to do the same. "You're saying you can just sever the bond if I walk away? It'll be that easy for you?"

His eyes glowed gold, and he let go of her hand only to grip her upper arms and bring her to his chest.

"It will kill me to let you go. Don't you get that? I don't want to lose you because of a stupid technicality."

Her heart raced, but she couldn't let him off the hook. She didn't know what he wanted, and until he was honest with the both of them, she couldn't make another mistake.

"You won't lose me because of that. You'll lose me because you didn't want me in the first place."

Quinn cursed and lowered his forehead to hers. "Gina, damn it. I'm not doing this right. I don't want you to fight Helena. I don't want Helena. I want you. If things had been different, if I hadn't mated with her in the first place, there would have been no doubt in my mind. I would have mated you in a heartbeat."

She couldn't believe her ears. Her throat went dry, and she tried to swallow. "But all of that did happen. And you got Jesse out of the deal."

He sighed. "Jesse's the most important thing in my life. You know that. Hell, you mated with me *because* of that. Gina, you're also right up there. You should have been up there in the first place, but I was too blind to see it."

She pulled back and stared up at him. "What are you saying, Quinn?"

He cupped her face, his eyes bright. "I don't want you to fight Helena because I've already made my choice. You're it for me, Gina. I don't want another mate. I want you. I want your strength, your heart, your loyalty, your beauty. I want it all. I'm a selfish bastard for wanting all of that without showing you that I'm a better man than I have been, but I can't help it. I love you, Gina. I want that forever that our bond promised, even if we tried to hide it."

She froze, her brain going in a hundred different directions.

"Quinn…"

His thumb caressed her cheek. "I know I went against the rules and fell in love with you, but I've never been good at following the rules when it comes to you. If I could take you and Jesse and run away from the Pack, I would, but I can't. We all need the bonds we've made. Our Pack needs us."

Tears slid down her cheeks, and he brushed them away. "You…you weren't supposed to love me. We said we wouldn't. We said we'd mate for Jesse, and that was it."

He nodded, the frown on his face making her ache. "I know. I will never be able to repay you for doing what you did to save Jesse's life, but I want to find a way to make this work between us. Fate might have put us together, but I want to be the one who helps *keep* us together."

She licked her lips, her wolf nudging at her to kiss her mate and seal the promise. She couldn't though. She couldn't think. It was all too much, and she couldn't believe it was real.

His face fell, and he took a step back. "But I understand if you don't want me. I don't deserve it. Jesse should be fine if we have to switch over the bond to Helena." His face looked like he sucked a raw lemon. "God, I hate that woman, but if you need to find yourself a mate you could love, one that you can fight for, I'll step back. I'm not going to go all Alpha on you and force you to love me. You deserve more than that."

Then he did something that truly awed her.

He lowered his head and bared his neck, giving her the upper hand, the dominance.

That this man would do this…she couldn't take it anymore.

She took two steps and cupped his face, forcing his gaze to hers. "Never bow to me, Quinn. You're a proud wolf, and you should remain that way. I was only hesitating because things are going so fast. I love you too. I know I shouldn't have fallen for you, but I couldn't help it. I want to know everything about you and fall in love with those parts too. Do you get that? I want you, Quinn, not some other fictional wolf I've never met."

He let out a breath and smiled, his eyes glowing with his wolf. "Gina…"

She smiled back then kissed his chin. "We're so freaking stupid, aren't we?"

He snorted then shook his head. "We're stupid for each other, that's for sure. I should have told you how I felt last night. In fact, I was working my way up to it, and then everything changed." His face sobered.

"I don't want you to have to fight in a mating circle, but with the way the Pack is right now, I don't see a way out."

She grinned. "I'll kick her ass, Quinn. I was never worried about losing. She's nothing compared to me. I was only worried that you didn't *want* me to win."

"I want you, Gina. All of you. Forever. Got me?"

She reached up and wrapped her arm around his neck, pulling her to him. "Yep. Now you've got me."

He pressed his lips to hers, and she opened for him, tangling her tongue with his. She moaned into him, gripping his shoulder with her free hand, wanting more of him. He pulled back, nipping at her lips, then her chin and neck. When she pressed her body tight against him, he growled then gripped her ass in his hands. He lifted her up, and she wrapped her legs around his waist, wanting him, craving him.

She licked and nipped at his skin, running her hands over his face, his shoulders, his back. He massaged her ass, rocking his hard cock along her pussy. Her body ached and warmed, wanting him inside her.

"If I can't fuck you right now, I think I'm going to go wolf and rip something apart," he growled.

She smiled then licked behind his ear, loving the way his body shook when he did. "Then fuck me. Against the wall, over the couch, in our bed. I don't care. Just get inside me."

Quinn slammed her back against the wall then reached between them for the button on her jeans. She whimpered, her body shaking.

"Sorry to interrupt, but you're both needed at the circle."

Gina froze as Gideon's voice pierced through her sexual haze.

Quinn growled then pulled back, his hands still on her ass. "Get. Out." His wolf was upfront, and Gina was worried he'd do something stupid—like challenge the Alpha of his Pack.

Gideon growled back, his eyes glowing gold. "Calm yourself, Quinn."

Gina patted Quinn's cheek and forced him to turn to her. "Let me knock this bitch off her pedestal, and then we can come back and finish what we started. Okay?"

Quinn lifted a lip in a snarl then visibly calmed himself, his shoulders lowering. He let out a shaky breath then let her fall to her feet. He took two steps back, his breathing labored.

"I apologize, Gideon. I was lost in the moment, and you came at a bad time."

She couldn't touch him to console him. If she did, she had a feeling they'd end up right back where they started, and that wouldn't end well for any of them.

"You have no idea how sorry I am for interrupting," Gideon said roughly. "If I could, I'd have let you two go at it, and I'd kick Helena off our lands. As it is, in order to make sure Shannon doesn't do anything else to circumvent my authority, I need to make sure this goes through without a hitch."

Quinn turned to Gideon, his head tilted, the action more wolf than man. "Then you'll kick Shannon's ass?"

Gideon snorted. "Not physically, but now that I know at least some of her plan, I can make sure the elders don't use any more power than they need. Meaning none at all in most cases. I don't like having my role as Alpha challenged by someone who has no right to do so." He met Gina's gaze. "I am truly sorry you're getting caught up in our Pack problems. It was never my intention."

She knew this was out of the Alpha's control. Every Pack had their own laws, their own issues. This was just one thing the Talons wouldn't let happen again.

"You're forgiven. There is something I will make clear though. I'm not going to kill Helena." At both men's looks, she shook her head. "I could kill her, but that will only make Shannon do something to take revenge against the Redwoods or Quinn. I can't have that. Plus, I won't be responsible for killing Jesse's mother."

"She's not his mother. She was an incubator who left her young when he was vulnerable."

Gina sighed at Quinn's words. "I get that. I do. If I felt Helena was at all sincere about her desire to get her son back, I'd feel differently, but I don't. What I don't want to do, though, is have Jesse see me as the woman who killed the mother he never knew. I won't take that onto my shoulders, and honestly, you can't make me."

Gideon nodded, pride in his eyes, while Quinn came to her side. He brushed his knuckles along her cheek.

"You're a good woman, Gina. I'm proud to call you mate."

She reached up and kissed his chin again. "You're a good man, Quinn. Never forget that." She let out a breath. "Now, let me go kick her ass and prove to Shannon she shouldn't mess with me." She frowned. "Have you called my parents about this?"

Quinn put his hand on her shoulder and squeezed.

"We told them," Gideon answered. "Finn is on his way to be here, but the others can't come."

She nodded, understanding. "You don't want to make it a Pack issue by having the Alpha and the rest of the inner circle here. I get it. As for Finn? Why is he coming? He's the Heir. He should stay home. I'll be okay."

Gideon merely raised a brow. "First, I can't exactly tell the Redwoods what to do. Yeah, this is my Pack, my den, my land, but I can't stop them from getting you and carting you away. It would start something. Not a war, but something none of us wants to deal with. The whole reason the two of you met was to ensure our Packs are working together. The fact that you two are even mated tells me we're on our way to making sure that happens. As for Finn? He's amazingly stubborn when it comes to people he cares about."

She grinned at the thought of her brother. "He's tougher than anyone I know, and I know a lot of tough wolves. I'm glad he's coming. That means that we're showing cooperation between the Packs without making it look like it's Pack against Pack."

"It wouldn't be anyway, considering Helena is not Pack." Gideon growled at that, and Gina had to agree with him.

"No, this is all about power plays and protection," Quinn added in.

"And when you finish kicking her ass, that will be the last time we hear about her," Gideon said, and Gina smiled.

"Then let's get to it. I'm not cocky, I'm confident," she said. "And I really want to get this over with." Her wolf perked up, ready to fight. She didn't know if they would be fighting as wolves or humans, but either way, she was ready. She had to be if she wanted to keep her mate thanks to archaic rules with loopholes that made no sense.

Quinn kissed her one more time, and then they were off. By the time they made it to the circle, Finn was standing with the Brentwoods.

She went to her brother and hugged him tight. "Thanks for coming."

"I shouldn't have had to come at all," he snapped. "This is ridiculous."

She rubbed his back then pulled away. "I love Quinn, Finn. I'm not going to let some bitch stop me."

Finn smiled full out, his eyes brightening. "No shit? You love him." He looked over her shoulder and growled. "And you? You love my sister? Because if you don't, I'm taking her home right now."

Gina closed her eyes and prayed for patience. God save her from dominant male wolves.

"I love her, Finn. You don't need to worry about that."

"Are you two done?" She opened her eyes and glared at each one.

Finn shrugged. "It'll be worse with Dad and Mark and the rest of them. Oh, and Mom? Yeah. This should be fun."

"One battle at a time, okay?" she asked, and Finn hugged her again.

"Okay. Now kick her ass because this is fucking ridiculous."

"Stop cursing," she teased, needing to lighten the moment.

"Mom's not here," Finn whispered, and she laughed.

Quinn came up from behind her and put his hand on her hip. She sighed and leaned into him, her wolf calming at the touch.

"Where's Brynn?" her mate asked Walker, who had come up to their party.

"She's with Jesse," the other man said. "She wanted to make sure he had a familiar face since he couldn't be here."

Gina looked up at Quinn, who nodded. "I'm glad she's there," he said.

"Brynn?" Finn asked. "That's your sister, right?"

Walker narrowed his eyes at her teenage brother. Finn might have technically been an adult, but in the eyes of someone well over a hundred, he was still a pup.

"Yes." With that short answer, Walker went back to the others.

"Did I say something wrong?" Finn asked, a smile on his face.

"Oh shut up. I don't have time for this." She grinned then looked out at the circle. "When do we start?"

Quinn leaned down and kissed her temple. "Soon, I hope. I don't know if Helena is here or not. We'll find out though."

"Is that her?" Finn asked, and Gina looked up.

"That's her," she growled.

Helena strode in, her hips swaying. Gone was the woman who looked contrite and apologetic. No, this was a woman on the prowl, a woman who wanted the man she'd left behind.

Well, too bad, because she couldn't have him.

"Since both wolves are here, and since we can't let the mate in question decide, we're ready to begin," Gideon said, his voice holding contempt.

"Since Helena is the wronged party, as her mate was stolen from her, she can decide if they fight as wolf or human," Shannon said.

Gina's jaw dropped as the wolves around her growled and shouted.

"Wronged?" Quinn yelled. "You've got to be kidding me. She's the one who left me. She's the one who almost killed me and Jesse. Fuck her. I want nothing to do with her. I've made my decision. It's Gina. It will *always* be Gina. No matter the outcome."

Gina's heart bloomed, and she gripped Quinn's hand and squeezed.

"I'll fight and win. You don't have to worry."

He turned and cupped her face before kissing her. Hard.

"I love you, Gina. I made my choice, and you're it. I don't trust her not to try something tricky."

She closed her eyes and inhaled his scent. It strengthened her while before it would have left her muddled and worried.

"I have something to fight for, Quinn. Something more than she could ever hope to have." She kissed him again, putting her heart into the kiss, into him. "I'm coming back to you."

"If you're quite done..." Shannon snapped.

"Watch your tone, wolf," Gideon said, his voice deadly calm.

Shannon glared then ran a hand over her dress. "What I meant was it was the *witch* who wronged her."

"Never trust a witch," Helena said, her voice snide.

"Fucking bitch," Finn snarled.

"Language, Finn," Gina snapped.

"Is this really the time?" he asked incredulously.

"No, but it's calming me, so get over it." She looked at Helena then dismissed her to face Shannon. "I'm a witch so you need to watch your tone. I'm not your wolf. I don't need to respect you. As for who wronged who, we all know what really happened. If you're in some kind of denial, that will be something we'll all deal with later." She looked over at Gideon. "Or maybe that's something you'll have to deal with on your own because I don't really care. Now, about the challenge? I don't care either. I'll fight as wolf or as human. We all know I'm stronger. If she tries *anything* that goes outside the rules, the entire Pack, as well as my brother, are here to judge." She narrowed her eyes at the elder. "Don't start a war you can't win."

With that, she kissed Quinn one more time, squeezed Finn's hand, and then strode into the circle.

She was a witch, a wolf, and a woman who loved a man who loved her back. She would one day be the Enforcer and had fought the prejudice of those who didn't think she was good enough for her blood and didn't like how she'd come into her powers.

She wouldn't lose today.

And from the look on Helena's face, the other woman knew it too.

"Human with claws," Helena spat. "We'll fight as human."

Gina cracked her knuckles and let her claws come through her fingertips. It was a hard shape to keep if the wolf wasn't strong enough. She didn't think Helena would be, but maybe the other woman thought she could handle it.

"Good enough for me." She kept her eyes on Helena just in case the other woman tried something. She wouldn't put it past her considering her background.

"As humans then," Gideon said. "Fight fair, and fight tough. Begin!"

Gina dodged right as Helena swiped at her. The other woman growled and snapped, trying to get at Gina, but Gina was faster. Helena clawed at her but Gina rolled out of the way. She used her right arm to grip Helena's upper arm and pull her close. The other woman screamed then bit at Gina's neck.

Freaking bitch.

She didn't want to prolong the fight; she wasn't a damn cat. Instead, she stepped up, wrapped her hand around Helena's neck, and flipped the other woman onto her back.

She slid her claws into the other woman's skin gently, careful not to nick an artery. "Yield," she growled, her voice low. "You have no say here. You were never going to win. He's mine. And you know what? He chose me, same as I chose him. Just go away and let us live."

Helena whimpered then slammed her palm into the ground twice.

The crowed erupted in cheers, and it was the first time Gina had heard them. She'd put all of that out of her mind while she was fighting. Now that the adrenaline was starting to leave her system, she just wanted to get out of there.

"Gina wins. Helena is forfeit," Gideon yelled.

"Wait!" Shannon screamed.

"Shut up," Gideon said. "You've had your say. Helena, you are hereby banished from the Pack and from the den. You've hurt this Pack enough."

With that, Helena screamed, but Gina didn't care. Others came to take care of the now banished woman—most likely to just kick her off Pack lands—but all Gina could scent or feel was Quinn as his arms wrapped around her.

"Mine," he growled before taking her lips.

She pulled away, gasping. "Mine."

He was hers, for forever and eternity.

Thank the goddess.

Chapter Twelve

Gina's back slammed into the wall again, and she screamed, wanting more. They'd just made it through the door, barely closing it behind them, when Quinn had pushed her against the wall and licked and sucked at her neck.

"Lock the damn door," she panted. "I don't want to be interrupted this time."

Quinn pulled back and grinned. "Take off your clothes before I shred them." He stomped to the door, snapped the lock closed, then started to strip. She had her shirt and bra off in the next breath. As she toed off her shoes, she worked on getting her pants off, her hands shaking.

"Next time I will peel you out of your clothes layer by layer and make it slow. Savor every bit."

She shivered at his words, at his promise.

"This time, though, I want you naked and spread out over my table. I can't wait anymore."

She cupped his face and kissed him, tangling her tongue with his. "Goddess, I've missed your cock."

He snorted then picked her up by the waist before depositing her on the table. She sucked in a breath at the coolness on her overheated skin. "You've had my cock once, Gina. How can you miss it?"

She rolled her eyes then reached out and gripped his length. He groaned and pumped into her hand. "I want more of you. I need more. Only once wasn't enough."

He kept thrusting his hips then lowered his head and kissed her.

"You can have me every day for the rest of our lives. How about that?"

"More than once sometimes?" she teased.

He pulled away then knelt between her legs and parted her thighs. "Anytime you want me. I'm yours."

She opened her mouth to say something then groaned as he licked her pussy in one long swipe. "Goddess help me, I love your mouth on me."

He hummed against her clit, and she wrapped her legs around his neck, pulling him closer. He kept his hands on her lips and lapped at her, spearing her with his tongue before biting down on her clit. Her breasts ached, and she leaned up on one arm so she could pinch her nipples, needing release. He licked her again, this time growling against her, and she let her head fall back, screaming his name as she came.

Quinn stood up before she came down off her high and entered her in one stroke. "Fuck, Gina. You're still so damn tight, and I can feel you squeeze me since you're still coming."

She licked her lips then reached up to cup his face. "Fuck me. Make love to me. Just do me. I don't really care what you thought, just *be* with me."

He kissed her hard then squeezed her hips in a bruising grip. "As you wish." He pulled out of her, and she whimpered at the loss. Before she could tell him to return, he slammed back into her, sending her body into overdrive. She gripped the edge of the table so he didn't knock her off then met his hips, thrust for thrust. Her breasts bounced, and her body ached from where he pistoned inside her, but she didn't care. She wanted more.

"Goddess, I love you."

He grinned then went faster. "Love you too, baby."

He leaned forward as she wrapped her legs around his waist. She kept up with him then moved to cup his face. The movement forced her to slide across the table, but her legs kept her stable. She had to touch him and couldn't hold back.

He held her close as he moved, pumping in and out of her, bringing them closer together as he rose along the crest.

"You're my witch, my wicked witch," he panted.

She met his gaze and let the tears fall at his words. The love in the word that had once hurt her made her fall in love with him all over again. She cupped his face, rocking her hips so she could feel every inch of him.

"You're my wicked wolf, Quinn. My wolf. My everything."

He kissed her then slammed into her once more. She came on a rush and felt him come inside her, filling her until they both lay panting on the table, their bodies sweat-slick and spent.

"This is going to be one hell of a ride," he murmured, holding her close.

"I wouldn't have it any other way," she said back, knowing it was the truth. They'd mated in the oddest of circumstances, but now they were united and together. She wouldn't change that for anything. The moon goddess had chosen right, even if Gina had doubted at first. Thank the goddess.

There were times to drool over a sexy wolf.

Staring at her mate across the table during a council meeting was totally one of them.

"If you two are quite done mooning over one another, are we ready to call it a day?" Parker asked, laughter in his voice.

Gina blushed, but Quinn looked unrepentant. "What were we saying?"

Parker rolled his eyes but didn't stop smiling. "We were saying that we're ready to set up the next phase of the council."

"Oh good. Sorry. I'll pay better attention."

Quinn coughed, and she kicked him. Jerk. Sexy jerk, but still a jerk.

"So the maternals are working well together then?" Quinn asked, his voice calm. See? Jerk.

"Yes, we've had meetings between the Redwoods and Talons to see what kinds of activities we can do together," Kimberly, the Talon maternal, said.

"And the security runs are going well," Lorenzo put in. "Nothing too dramatic, but we're starting to trust each other a bit more."

"It'll take time," Gina put in. "But it's a start."

"As for our next meeting, you're going to need another Talon," Quinn said, and Gina's heart warmed.

Lorenzo grinned. "Yeah, since you're going all Redwood with your mate."

Gina smiled. She couldn't help it. Jesse was officially healthy enough to go through the process of becoming a Redwood. It would hurt Quinn when he broke the bond, if only for a moment, but Kade and Gideon would shield Jesse from the pain. It was what they could do for the children. Now Jesse was a little ball of energy running around as though he didn't have a care in the world. Gina wouldn't have changed any choices she'd made on the path of Jesse's health and her mating. It had been rocky as hell, but it was so worth it.

She still remembered the way Quinn and Jesse had become part of her whole family.

Gina had held her breath, praying to the goddess that everything would work out. It wasn't like either of them could *really* kill one another.

Right?

Her father had folded his arms over his chest, not blinking.

Quinn had held his arms at his side, apparently trying to look non-threatening.

"You hurt her. I'll kill you." Her dad hadn't smiled when he said it so she'd known it was the truth.

Quinn had nodded solemnly. "Of course. But if I hurt her, she'll get first dibs at killing me."

Her dad had smiled then and lowered his arms. Before Gina could hit Quinn for his remark, Kade had lowered himself to his knee to talk to Jesse.

Apparently the whole dominant-male thing where they threatened death made them family.

Who knew.

"I'm going to step away from the council," Gina put in, and Parker sighed. "I have to. I'm going to be shadowing Adam more and more, and Quinn can take over my spot."

"I think Max Brentwood, Gideon's cousin, would be a good replacement for me," Quinn said. "I'll ask him and Gideon if the rest of you agree."

Lorenzo and Kimberly nodded. "We're fine with that," Kimberly said. "Though, Gina, we don't want to lose you completely. After all, you're a founding member of the Council of the Northwest Packs. You can't get rid of us that easily."

"I'll be around, but I think you guys are on the right track."

"The next step, of course, is to make sure that *other* Packs around the United States are on similar pages," Parker put in.

Gina let out a breath. "We've always held the same laws of the moon goddess, but the Packs around the country have never been united before."

Parker shook his head. "We're not going to form one Pack between the Redwoods and the Talons, and we sure won't be doing that with the entirety of the wolf civilization, but from what Kade and Gideon are saying, we're going to need to find a way to work together. Just in case."

Something was coming. They all felt it. They just didn't know what it was. Forming trust and alliances between the two Packs was only the first step. It wasn't going to be easy and sure as hell wouldn't be fast, but they'd find a way to ensure the safety of their race.

They were wolves, after all, and they were stronger than most. They hadn't lived this long for nothing.

In fact, all the wolves were being extra cautious. Helena had been sent off Pack lands, but they would be keeping an eye out for her. She had confessed later that she'd only wanted to come back for the protection. It made sense considering lone wolves were becoming scarcer. It was harder for them to live in the human world without the Pack's protection. Helena had wanted a home and she had gone about it the wrong way. While Gina didn't want the other woman to die at the hands of those who might want to hurt her, she couldn't really put much effort into wanting Helena as part of *either* Pack.

After they finished their meeting, they said their good-byes and headed outside. Gina leaned into Quinn's hold, inhaling his scent.

"How does it feel to have finished your final council meeting as a Talon?" she asked as they walked to their car.

Quinn stopped her then kissed her softly. "It feels like I'm with my mate, and that's all that matters." He cupped her face and grinned. She loved when he smiled. He hadn't done it when they'd first met, and now he did it all the time.

"You ready to go home and make sure we're mated?" she teased.

Quinn's eyes darkened, and he nipped her lip. "You have the best come-on, witch."

"What should I have said? Do me?"

"That would have worked too," he said then picked her up.

She squealed then wrapped her legs around his waist. "I'm so glad I came to that council meeting even though I was scared to death about going."

Quinn met her gaze and licked his lips. "I'm glad you came as well. No matter what happens with the Packs, it's you and me. We'll figure out the rest as we go, but we're a unit."

Her wolf nudged at her, content in the arms of their mate. "Forever, my wicked wolf."

"Forever, my wicked witch."

Next up in the Redwood Pack and Talon Pack World:
Tattered Loyalties

Sign up for the 1001 Dark Nights Newsletter
and be entered to win a Tiffany Key necklace.

There's a new contest every month!

Go to www.1001DarkNights.com to subscribe.

As a bonus, all subscribers will receive a free
1001 Dark Nights story
The First Night
by Lexi Blake & M.J. Rose

Turn the page for a full list of the
1001 Dark Nights fabulous novellas...

1001 Dark Nights

WICKED WOLF by Carrie Ann Ryan
A Redwood Pack Novella

WHEN IRISH EYES ARE HAUNTING by Heather Graham
A Krewe of Hunters Novella

EASY WITH YOU by Kristen Proby
A With Me In Seattle Novella

MASTER OF FREEDOM by Cherise Sinclair
A Mountain Masters Novella

CARESS OF PLEASURE by Julie Kenner
A Dark Pleasures Novella

ADORED by Lexi Blake
A Masters and Mercenaries Novella

HADES by Larissa Ione
A Demonica Novella

RAVAGED by Elisabeth Naughton
An Eternal Guardians Novella

DREAM OF YOU by Jennifer L. Armentrout
A Wait For You Novella

STRIPPED DOWN by Lorelei James
A Blacktop Cowboys ® Novella

RAGE/KILLIAN by Alexandra Ivy/Laura Wright
Bayou Heat Novellas

DRAGON KING by Donna Grant
A Dark Kings Novella

PURE WICKED by Shayla Black
A Wicked Lovers Novella

HARD AS STEEL by Laura Kaye
A Hard Ink/Raven Riders Crossover

STROKE OF MIDNIGHT by Lara Adrian
A Midnight Breed Novella

ALL HALLOWS EVE by Heather Graham
A Krewe of Hunters Novella

KISS THE FLAME by Christopher Rice
A Desire Exchange Novella

DARING HER LOVE by Melissa Foster
A Bradens Novella

TEASED by Rebecca Zanetti
A Dark Protectors Novella

THE PROMISE OF SURRENDER by Liliana Hart
A MacKenzie Family Novella

FOREVER WICKED by Shayla Black
A Wicked Lovers Novella

CRIMSON TWILIGHT by Heather Graham
A Krewe of Hunters Novella

CAPTURED IN SURRENDER by Liliana Hart
A MacKenzie Family Novella

SILENT BITE: A SCANGUARDS WEDDING by Tina Folsom
A Scanguards Vampire Novella

DUNGEON GAMES by Lexi Blake
A Masters and Mercenaries Novella

AZAGOTH by Larissa Ione
A Demonica Novella

NEED YOU NOW by Lisa Renee Jones
A Shattered Promises Series Prelude

SHOW ME, BABY by Cherise Sinclair
A Masters of the Shadowlands Novella

ROPED IN by Lorelei James
A Blacktop Cowboys ® Novella

TEMPTED BY MIDNIGHT by Lara Adrian
A Midnight Breed Novella

THE FLAME by Christopher Rice
A Desire Exchange Novella

CARESS OF DARKNESS by Julie Kenner
A Dark Pleasures Novella

Also from Evil Eye Concepts:

TAME ME by J. Kenner
A Stark International Novella

THE SURRENDER GATE By Christopher Rice
A Desire Exchange Novel

About Carrie Ann Ryan

New York Times and *USA Today* Bestselling Author Carrie Ann Ryan never thought she'd be a writer. Not really. No, she loved math and science and even went on to graduate school in chemistry. Yes, she read as a kid and devoured teen fiction and Harry Potter, but it wasn't until someone handed her a romance book in her late teens that she realized that there was something out there just for her. When another author suggested she use the voices in her head for good and not evil, The Redwood Pack and all her other stories were born.

Carrie Ann is a bestselling author of over twenty novels and novellas and has so much more on her mind (and on her spreadsheets *grins*) that she isn't planning on giving up her dream anytime soon.

Visit Carrie Ann online at http://carrieannryan.com/.

Tattered Loyalties
Talon Pack, Book 1
By Carrie Ann Ryan
Coming February 17, 2015

Gideon shrugged out of his clothes then stepped into his shower, letting the hot water pound down his back. His muscles ached from the fight and the tension of the unknown.

He closed his eyes and spoke loudly over the hum of the water. "We're going to talk about plans to come out to the public. Or at least, plans to make plans. Then we're going to make sure our underground tunnels are in shape since the connection between the two packs is relatively new."

No one knew what would happen once the humans found out about the existence of shifters, and demons. They'd been planning for years, though, on the eventual outcome where they'd have to protect themselves from people who didn't understand and feared what they didn't know.

He let out a breath and quickly soaped up, knowing he was running late. Between the lone wolves trying to find a way to stay alive, his Pack watching him more than usual for some reason, and this meeting, he needed a damned weekend off.

He was the Alpha, however, so he knew that would never happen.

He shut off the water and got out so he could get ready for the meeting. Walker had left him alone, thankfully, and he quickly pulled on a long-sleeved cotton shirt and jeans. With any other Alpha, he'd put on something a little more formal, but this was Kade and his family—Gideon could go with a little comfort and be okay.

When he walked out to his living room to pull on his boots, he sighed. He knew they were there of course, but his wolf wasn't in the mood to deal with his entire family in one room.

"I suppose just meeting me at chambers would have been too much for all of you?"

"You love us, brother dearest," Brynn, his sister and the lone Brentwood female, teased from her perch on the edge of the couch.

Gideon pinched the bridge of his nose. "No seriously. Why are you all here?"

"Because you need us," Brandon, his youngest brother and the Talon Omega, said from the couch.

"Do I really need you here?" he asked, knowing he was fighting a lost cause.

"Of course," Max, his cousin, answered. "We're all going to the meeting anyway, why not go together?"

"We're one big happy family," Mitchell said dryly.

"What they aren't saying is that we're worried about you," Kameron, his brother and Enforcer, added in.

Gideon growled while Ryder closed his eyes and cursed.

"Really, Kameron?" Ryder put in. "I thought we had a plan."

Gideon stiffened. "A plan? Why the hell would you need a plan to deal with me? Why are you *here*?"

Brynn stood up and walked toward him. She brushed her long, dark brown hair—the same color as the rest of the Brentwoods—behind her shoulders and blinked up at him with the Brentwood blue eyes.

"You're our brother and you're hurting," she whispered. They were all wolves so they could hear her clearly. "You had to kill a lone wolf who threatened the border and wouldn't back down. Now you're having to make decisions that, as we see it, won't have an easy outcome. So, Gideon, brother mine, brother ours, we're here for you. Even if we annoy you to no end. We're here."

Gideon narrowed his eyes, even as his heart warmed at her words. Yeah, his siblings and cousins were there for him, but some things were meant for only the Alpha. If he had a mate, he'd be able to lean on her just a little, but since the goddess hadn't blessed him, he didn't have that option.

At this point, he wasn't sure he ever would.

On that depressing thought, he led his family out of his home and headed toward the meeting room. He wanted to get this over with. It wasn't like they were going to get anything done anyway. They couldn't. Not with the rest of the Packs in the US keeping silent. Parker, the Voice of the Wolves, was on a mission at the moment searching for the other Packs and trying to convince them to talk to Gideon and Kade, but Gideon didn't hold out high hopes. Parker was a Redwood, the biological son of a mass murderer, even if he'd been adopted into the Redwood family.

Some wolves just couldn't see past that, and Gideon was worried that might hurt their chances of finding a way to make all of the Packs work together. However, he could only work on one problem at a time.

They made their way as a group to the other side of the den where the Redwoods would be entering the woods. They had to go past the sentries at the wards to be let through, but most of them had done it before. Actually, Gideon wasn't sure who Kade was bringing.

The Redwoods were in the middle of a shift in hierarchy. The younger Jamensons were taking over for their parents slowly but surely. That meant that Kade would be bringing any number of his powerhouse to the table. It didn't really matter since Gideon had met most of them and liked those he'd met. Not that he'd tell them that. No, he was still the grumpy, badass Alpha to the outside world.

It worked for him.

Kade come up first, a small smile on his face. With so many people and coming into a different den, the ceremony of walking to a meeting was a little ridiculous, and both of them knew it. It had to be done though.

Kade had brought his mate, Melanie, as well as both sets of Betas, Omegas, and Healers with him. He'd left the Enforcers at home to protect the den with countless other wolves apparently. Interesting, but it made sense. As the younger generation came into their powers, they were learning from the older generation. It would be interesting to see how they reacted in the future when the older generation, Kade's brothers, had to step down fully.

He'd also brought his Heir, his son Finn, with him, which made sense.

He'd also brought another wolf with him. A younger woman who, from the look of her, was a Jamenson, but Gideon wasn't sure he'd ever met her. Her long chestnut brown hair flowed over her shoulders, blowing slightly in the wind. She wasn't small. No, she was at least of average height, but where most of the wolves in front of her were all muscle and strength, her body held curves and a softness he didn't see in most wolves.

Odd, he thought he'd met most, if not all the Jamensons.

Her cheekbones angled high and her plump lips thinned into a line when she looked at him. She tilted her head and blinked up at him with bright green eyes and he froze, his wolf howling.

Shocked, he almost took a step back, but it was only because of his strength as Alpha that he didn't.

Mate.

That scent, that pull on his wolf.

Mate.

"Gideon, Brentwoods," Kade said, his voice deep. "I think you've met most of us before. Probably not Brie, though. Brie, these are the

Brentwoods. Brentwoods, this is Jasper and Willow's daughter, my niece, Brie."

She smiled softly, but her eyes were only on him, not on the rest of the Pack or her family. In fact, he was only looking at her, not at Kade or the others.

Holy shit.

He'd just found his mate and she was a fucking Redwood.

And from the way her wolf reached out to his, she was a submissive as well.

A Talon Alpha and a Redwood submissive?

Yeah, fate royally sucked.

On behalf of 1001 Dark Nights,

Liz Berry and M.J. Rose would like to thank ~

Steve Berry
Doug Scofield
Kim Guidroz
Jillian Stein
Dan Slater
Asha Hossain
Chris Graham
Pamela Jamison
Jessica Johns
Richard Blake
BookTrib After Dark
and Simon Lipskar